BETRAYAL III

A. MARIE

MW00986796

© 2020 A. Marie

ISBN# 978-1-7350337-2-3

All rights reserved. Without limiting the rights under copyright reserved above. No part of this book may be reproduced, stored in or introduced into a retrieval system, or transmitted in any form, or by any means (electronic, mechanical, photocopying, recording, or otherwise) without prior written consent from the author except brief quotes used in reviews, interviews or magazines. This is a work of fiction. It is not meant to depict, portray or represent any particular real person. All the characters, incidents and dialogue in this written work are the product of the author's imagination and are not to be considered as real. Any references or similarities to actual events, entities, real people living or dead, or to real locations are intended for the sole purpose of giving this novel a sense of reality. Any similarities with other names, characters, entities, places, people or incidents are entirely coincidental.

CONTENTS

DEDICATION & ACKNOWLEDGMENTS

Vicky, you are probably going to kill me for this... but oh well! Big shout out to you for truly being my number one fan. You would text me in the middle of the night because these characters are on your brain. They don't let you sleep just like they don't allow me to some nights. Thank you for always being my other brain. You've pushed me in ways you wouldn't even know. I will always be grateful for you and again this is dedicated to you.

To all my supporters, y'all have no idea what it means to me to have the amount of love and support you have shown me throughout this journey. You guys took a chance on me as a first-time author and haven't given up on me since. I am forever grateful for you all. To my tribe, I love you ladies with everything in me. To my favorite editor, B you already know what it is. Thank you from the bottom of my heart for seeing something in me and walking with me through this hand in hand. As I always say you are a real one sis. To my favorite author, the woman I call a gem, Ashley Antoinette. I give the biggest thanks to you. Thank you for the support and love you have shown me since day one. Thank you for aspiring me to be who I am destined to be. Love you down Twin.

Now, I hope you all are ready for this ride because whew, it is truly about to be something. Enjoy Ladies and Gents....

CHAPTER 1

*B*ANG. BANG. BANG.

"G mommy!"

Leah woke abruptly, screaming her godmother's name as the sound of gun shots resounded loudly in her ears. She looked around frantically as sweat trickled down her face. It was as if she was still standing at the club watching Dominic hang from the window of the car, letting off shots. Spraying whatever or whoever was in sight, hoping the bullet with Leah's name on it reached her. He was seeking revenge because he was certain Leah had something to do with the disappearance of his love. Her nightmare wasn't a nightmare, it was her reality. She was in Toledo Hospital as she laid around waiting on Stacy to come out of surgery. She was numb, her mind raced as the last words her godmother spoke played ping pong in her brain. *He's not who you think he is. What did she mean?* she thought. The day her real mother popped up and had told her to ask Stacy who the little light skin mutha-fucka she was running around town with played in her mind as well. Leah couldn't think straight. Everything about who he truly was, was starting to cause her mind to wander. Who was he? How did both of these women know who he was, but she didn't? Had he and Stacy been together before, a one night-stand? Leah's mind was all over the place as she pulled her phone out to call Jamison.

Leah needed him and not only did she need him, she needed answers. *Pick up*, she thought. She allowed the phone to ring five times before she hung up. When Leah looked up, there Jamison was sauntering in the hospital with Tyson and NuNu in tow. She sprinted from where she laid and rushed into his arms. Leah slammed into his body causing him to stumble back. She needed the shield that he always provided.

"Jamison."

Jamison picked her up, holding her close as if he were afraid, she just might disappear. He fisted her hair as he buried his face in the crook of her neck. Leah began to cry as she clung to him wrapping her legs around his waist as tight as she could. Her cries caused Jamison's eyes to mist. He felt her hurt. He knew at this very moment that her stomach was twisting and turning because his was too.

"Don't cry sweetie," he whispered, forcing Leah to look at him.

"Everything is going to be fine."

Leah looked to NuNu.

"My god son okay?" she asked.

NuNu nodded before Tyson pulled her back in the opposite direction, giving Leah and Jamison some space and privacy.

Jamison pecked Leah's lips and then her forehead. His assurance relaxed her. Her shield, it never failed. The elevators next to them opened and out walked Lena. She stepped off the elevators looking beautiful. She was dressed to impress but none of that mattered. Beauty was skin deep, but Lena's ways made her the ugliest sight known to man. Even with skintight denim jeans and a white V-neck shirt with white pumps to match, she still was hideous. Lena strolled past NuNu and Tyson making her way to where Leah and Jamison stood. NuNu looked her up and then down with disgust.

"I should slap fire from this bitch." She mumbled.

Tyson looked at her and pulled her in close.

"Chill lor mama." He whispered. NuNu bit into her bottom lip as she fought back the urge to lay hands on the woman who had abandoned her best friend. The woman who had come back into Leah's life causing hell. It had been months since they saw Lena and her presence wasn't welcomed. Leah had told her that she was dead to her and she meant every word. There was no reason why she should be showing up.

"She does anything to upset my boo and I'm rocking her old ass, Ty."

NuNu's voice held nothing but truth. It wasn't a threat, but a promise that she would make good on. Tyson knew that she always cashed in on the check that her ass was writing. He shook his head and hoped that everyone remained level-headed in a time like this. He was sure that Stacy wouldn't want anything else to take place, enough had transpired for one day. He grabbed NuNu by the waist, pulling her into him and kissed the tip of her nose. He needed to distract her from the presence of this woman because if he didn't, he knew she would act a fool about her best friend.

Lena approached Leah and Jamison. She looked at them and cleared her throat. They hadn't noticed her when she first stepped off the elevators. They hardly ever noticed anyone when in the presence of each other. It was like they were trapped in a bubble together and no one else mattered. When Leah turned to face her the sight of Lena instantly sickened her. Leah looked her up and down, turning her nose up like she was a foul smell that had invaded her nostrils. Leah had no respect for the woman who gave her life because she had made Leah's life hell.

"What are you doing here?" Leah asked. Irritation was laced in her tone as her stare penetrated the woman who gave her away to the next woman.

"Leah, I didn't come here for all that. Is Stephanie okay?" Lena asked, dismissing the attitude Leah was giving off.

Leah stared at her. She didn't have an answer for her and even if she did, she wasn't about to extend one to her. Lena rolled her eyes and then looked to Jamison. She smirked as she looked back and forth between the two. Lena shook her head as amusement danced in her eyes. Leah noticed the look and immediately thought of the day she had thrown Jamison in her face.

"What the fuck is so funny? Cause I want to laugh too!" Leah yelled.

"Sweetie, calm down," Jamison commanded. He wasn't sure who this woman was, but he wasn't with the drama. He had a lot running rapidly through his mind about the woman they were all waiting to hear good news about.

"You better listen to him, before I say some shit to hurt your feelings with your disrespectful ass," Lena said.

Leah's entire face frowned up as she cocked her head back. *Who the fuck this bitch thinks she talking to?* She thought as she bit down into her bottom lip. Leah steepled her two pointer fingers together, brought them to her lips and then pointed them at her birth mother. She wasn't with the threatening. Leah didn't like the fact that this woman who had once called herself a mother had the nerve to seem as if she had something hanging over her head.

"Hurt my feelings, you couldn't possibly hurt them any more than you have the day you let your bitch ass boyfriend's son rape me and then sent me away to my grandmother's house instead of making him leave. So, what the fuck do you got to say, Lena? Huh, cause I'm sure nothing else could hurt worse than that."

Jamison peered down at Leah and his heart cracked instantly. He closed his eyes and shook his head. He felt as if he had just been punched in the gut it twisted so bad. This was a part of Leah that he didn't know. They had never got the chance to dig that deep into their past. Hearing this awful story wounded him and his eyes began to water. His sweetie had endured something no one should ever go through. Jamison pulled her in close, not allowing another word to be spoken. He wrapped long arms around her and squeezed. He knew she was hurt because he felt her pain. Leah plowed her face into his chest as she shook her head from the memory and the audacity of Lena.

NuNu came out of nowhere. She ran up on Lena, yanked her by the back of the shirt, and sent her crashing to the floor. NuNu had told Tyson if Leah got upset that she was on Lena's ass and she meant just that. As soon as Leah was finished speaking, NuNu saw red.

"Nu'Asia!" Tyson barked. His calls for her went unheard. NuNu was serving Lena an ass whooping that had been well overdue.

"Bitch, I told you that I'd give you big bitch problems." NuNu said as she cocked her fist back and punched Lena in the mouth. NuNu pulled back a bloody fist and then punched her ass again. Lena had all that mouth but couldn't make good on her words when it came to NuNu. NuNu was teaching this old hoe a new school lesson. Tyson tried his best to get her off the woman but the death grip she had on Lena's shirt made it hard for him to restrain her. NuNu held on so tight that when he pulled her up, she pulled Lena right up with her tagging her, as Lena tried to fight her off.

Jamison stepped in to assist. Leah ran up. *TAG*. It was her turn to teach because Lena had failed as a mother and needed a lesson better yet, two and what better two teachers than

Leah and NuNu. Tyson and Jamison both could have sworn they saw the girls slap hands as if they were truly tag teaming this woman.

Jamison picked Leah up trying to stop the commotion. As he was scooping her up Leah kicked Lena in the head.

"Bitch!"

Tears streamed down Leah's face. It was pissing her off. She didn't want to shed tears. Not over someone who was undeserving of them. However, she had so much hatred built up for Lena that it all came pouring out. It was like Lena had cut Leah's pot from simmer all the way up to boil the moment she let the last statement slip from her mouth. Lena had betrayed her, had failed to protect the life she created and now Leah was letting it all out. Letting out every bit of hurt she had ever felt and every bit of resentment. She had always heard that betrayal hurt the most when it comes from someone you never expected. Leah would have never guessed that her own mother would ever damage her the way that she had. The hurt that Leah felt was indescribable it hurt that bad.

Lena stood staggering as she spit blood from her mouth. She couldn't believe the girls had jumped her. She didn't know that they moved as one. They weren't plural. Never plural, they were always singular and just handed Lena a single ass whooping. Together. You couldn't say Leah without saying NuNu, they were so close.

"Both you bitches got it coming!" She yelled as she tried to attack NuNu. Tyson turned and the stare he gave her stopped her dead in her tracks. He was never the one to condone this type of drama. It was silly to him, but when it came to his lady, he would rock anyone. Leah's mama wasn't exempt, she was subject to whatever as well when it came to NuNu, even Leah. Lena knew it was in her best interest to stop. The look on Tyson's face let her know that he wasn't the one to be tried.

She was outnumbered. However, she wouldn't be Lena if she didn't spread the fire before she left.

"Ma'am don't try it," he said. His voice was calm but firm. She burned holes in NuNu and then turned to face Leah.

"You helped your friend lay hands on me? I'm your fucking mama!"

"You're not shit to me!" Leah yelled

"My mama in the fucking operating room!"

Leah's words stung but like a boxer, Lena shook it off and went for the knockout.

"If that's your mama then why you fucking her son?"

Jamison, Tyson, and NuNu all looked in shock as the words Lena spoke shot Leah in the chest. Leah's eyes widened as she looked at Jamison and then back to Lena. She had to look down at her chest because she just knew Lena's words had just blown a hole through it.

"Yeah, this pretty muthafucka is Stephanie's son. So why you are running around here thinking she just the world's best mother, ask her why she didn't tell you she had a son that she gave up and now letting you fuck him?" Lena said with a hand on her hip and an eyebrow raised.

"And by the looks of it, you look pregnant bitch."

Leah took off. She was like the Tasmanian devil the way she had ran up on Lena.

"Bitch, keep his fucking name out your mouth!" Leah barked as she punched Lena in the nose.

"You lying ass hoe!"

Jamison scooped Leah up over his shoulder. He looked at Lena and pointed a finger in her direction.

"Leah, that's enough sweetie," he ordered. To see mother and daughter go at it, the way they were, pained him. They should be best friends but because of the things Leah had endured had caused a divide between the two women. They were fighting and calling each other names as if they were strangers out on the street.

"And lady I don't know who the fuck you think I am, but this ain't that. Keep my name out your mouth, cause you don't fucking know me."

Lena laughed mockingly. They were all clueless. Lena began to backpedal once she saw security approaching. They had been called by a staff member that had heard the commotion.

"I know yo ass well Jamison Semaj Banks. You were born September 21, 1978 and yo ass was adopted. Stephanie is your birth mama." She spat.

Jamison and Leah both looked at each other in stun. There was no way she could have known that. However, Leah knew her mother was petty. She knew Lena must have done her homework on Jamison, but she just couldn't believe that he was Stacy's son. She knew her godmother would have said something.

Lena was escorted out once everyone else was verified as the family of Stacy's. The information Lena spit out before departing had Jamison's head clouded. He didn't know Lena, but she seemed to know almost everything about him. Everything that he had been wanting to know. He looked to Leah who looked at him with the same confusion that he was feeling. Neither wanted to believe what was said, but damn if her words weren't making sense. Perfect sense. She knew too much and the only person that could confirm any of the accusations was in surgery at this very moment.

"Do you think she's telling the truth?" Leah whispered.

Leah had to ask. She had to know if he was thinking the same things she was. Jamison had no words as Lena's words were on repeat in his mind. Leah's mind flashed back to her godmother's last words before she became unconscious.

He's not who you think he is.

CHAPTER 2

"*P*arty of Stacy Gray."

The doctor called from the double doors of the waiting room. Leah's head snapped in his direction. They had been waiting for hours after the chaos that had taken place. Everyone sat in silence, each one wrapped in their own thoughts regarding the day's events. Leah took hurried steps in the doctor's direction, as nerves ate away at her with each step. She didn't know why her heart was pounding but it felt like it was trying to burst from her chest. They had all been waiting around in silence. The tension in the waiting room was thick, as everyone's minds wandered. The fighting and the accusations were all too much, but now they were finally about to get answers.

"Yes, that's my mother."

Leah's voice was shaky, barely audible as her eyes misted. She wasn't sure what was getting ready to come out of the doctor's mouth, but she was scared. Jamison, always able to sense her agony stepped up behind her and wrapped strong arms around her. Leah let out an audible breath. Her shield. He was there to provide instant comfort when she needed it.

"Your mother, is going to be fine. She was hit in the shoulder. We were able to remove the bullet and stitch her up. There is some nerve damage however, she'll be fine."

Leah couldn't contain her tears as she let out a sigh of relief.

"Thank God." She said. Leah wiped her face and then felt a gentle squeeze from Jamison.

"Can we see her?" Leah asked.

The doctor nodded and then smiled.

"Yes, she is asking for you and a Jamison." He said looking down at his clipboard.

Leah turned, facing Jamison. Jamison looked at the doctor and then down to Leah who was staring at him, waiting for him to respond. He had heard the statement that left Stacy's lips before she passed out and was confused. He was bothered as hell as to what she meant by him not being who Leah thought he was. There was silence as everyone waited for Jamison to respond.

"JJ you have to see what's up."

That was Tyson intervening, finally breaking the silence. Jamison had told him and NuNu both about what was said. They all were wanting to know what she meant. Jamison was everything. The most solid dude that any of them had come across. He was who he was and that was a certified solid ass nigga.

Jamison nodded and then allowed the doctor to lead the way. He and Leah walked hand and hand as they trailed the doctor down the hall. They approached Stacy's room and knocked before entering. When they walked in Stacy was lying in the bed, looking as if she were asleep. Leah crept in quietly and Jamison followed behind her. She pulled a chair up that was next to the bed and took a seat as she grasped Stacy's hand. Right away Stacy began to lift heavy eyelids.

"G mommy," Leah called out as she stood and kissed her forehead.

Stacy placed teary eyes on Jamison. They were now

having a stare down. She could no longer fight the tears that were threatening to fall. They slid down her face freely as her chest began to rock from the sight of him. Leah noticed the tense moment and could no longer hold back what she was wanting to ask her godmother.

"G mommy, what's going on?" Leah asked as she continued to look back and forth between the two. Seeing them together in this moment made Leah's heart race. Could Lena's words be true? *God is he her son?* Leah thought.

"G mommy, say something, is what Lena saying true? she said that Jamison is your son."

Leah looked to Jamison and then to her godmother trying to compare looks, hoping that she didn't see a resemblance.

Jamison laid eyes on Leah. Confusion written all over his face still. He then focused back on Stacy, staring hard. He walked up on the bed and grasped her hand. The sparks that spread through him was soul stirring. His heart began to beat rapidly and immediately swelled.

"G mommy!" Leah yelled as she witnessed the intense moment. *What the fuck is going on?*

Stacy held on tight to Jamison's hand as she rolled watering eyes toward her goddaughter. What she was about to reveal was going to be the hardest thing she would ever tell her goddaughter. This truth would surely cause a divide. A divide that she didn't want but delaying what was being asked was inevitable. Stacy lifted the bed slightly, wincing from the pain as she began to speak.

"I don't know any other way to say this other than to just say it. But Jamison…" Stacy paused as the words in her throat began to crack. She shook her head as flashes of the saddest day of her life ran through her mind. She shook the thought and then swiped at the single tear that slid down her face.

"Jamison what?" he and Leah both said in unison.

"Jamison, I'm the woman who gave you life."

Leah gasped, bringing both hands to her mouth. Jamison's

stomach plummeted. He snatched his hand away as he stumbled back. He could no longer keep his emotions from erupting from him. Leah watched in shock, not believing what was being said. This had to be a joke. Her g mommy didn't have any kids. Stacy had never spoke about having kids and here she was claiming that her man, her love was her god brother. Leah doubled over as nausea swept over her. She ran to the sink as the contents of her stomach came spewing from her.

Jamison backpedaled bumping into a cart as he put distance in between him and Stacy. He looked to see Leah at the sink, releasing the contents in her stomach. Though his heart was screaming for him to go to her, he resisted and rushed out the room. Stacy called for him. She screamed for him to come back. Her heart was in half as she watched her son rush out the room. She looked to see Leah heaving as she splashed water on her face. Her son was gone and now only her baby girl was left. Stacy hoped like hell that Leah didn't rush out of the room as well. She knew once she revealed the truth things would start to crumble and it was doing just that.

Leah looked from the sink, with disappointment in her eyes. She reached for a paper towel and patted her face as she walked back toward Stacy, taking a seat in the chair that sat next to her bed. Neither of them was able to speak as they just sat looking at each other, not knowing what to say. After a few minutes, Leah could no longer take the silence.

"G mommy explain this to me. You never said you had kids, so how is Jamison yours?"

Stacy looked at Leah, eyes burning with tears that slid down her face effortlessly as her mind went back to the day, she gave birth to Jamison. She inhaled a deep breath and released it slowly as she began to tell Leah everything that had happened. She didn't leave not one detail out because she needed Leah to feel everything. Stacy needed her to understand the logic behind her decision and why she couldn't raise her baby boy. They talked for hours, shedding tears as they clung to one another. By the time Stacy was done, Leah had developed a deeper love for her godmother and an even stronger bond was created.

Jamison burst through the doors of the waiting room, storming past Tyson and NuNu. Tyson stood immediately noticing the look of hurt and devastation on his brother's face. He knew that whatever had just been said in the room with Stacy and Leah couldn't have been good. Jamison was so mad he was a shade of red and his eyebrows dipped low. He looked like an angry pitbull the way his forehead was wrinkled up.

"JJ, what's wrong dummy?"

Tyson tried to grab Jamison by the arm as he brushed past. Jamison yanked away from his grasp and turned on his heels.

"Stacy is my fucking mom's dawg. She's my fucking birth mom." His voice cracked as he doubled over in grief. He placed hands to his knees and shook his head. Jamison was usually hard, never showed emotion. The only time he displayed signs of being soft is when he was in front of a woman he loved. However, his brother was witnessing him crumble. The hurt and anger he had behind Stacy's words were almost paralyzing him. He was stuck. Tyson pulled Jamison in and he released all emotions as he cried from the bottom of his soul. Jamison had always wondered what his birth mother looked like, he always dreamed of the day of actually getting to meet the woman who created him. He never thought in a million years that he would be meeting her under these circumstances. It had taken for him to fall in love with Leah to find her. She had abandoned him to play mommy to the next person. The person who now held the keys to his heart.

Tyson looked at Jamison stunned.

"Damn. I'm sorry JJ." He whispered.

NuNu stood in shock from the realization, that Lena's accusation was in fact to be true. Her eyes misted as her mind instantly went to Leah. She could only imagine how her best friend was feeling. She wanted to go to her, but something told her to just give her time and that Leah would seek her when she needed her.

Jamison broke the embrace and sniffed back his emotions, trying to restore his hard exterior. He looked at NuNu and then shook his head.

"You bet not ever tell nobody you seen me like this or I'm going to fuck your little ass up." He said playfully. They all shared a laugh and then there was silence amongst them. Jamison's mind was running a mile a minute and the rest of him couldn't keep up because he was still stuck. He was still in disbelief. A part of him wanted to go back to the room and talk to her. His heart was begging him to go back in that room and check on his sweetie and get answers from Stacy. There were so many questions that were jumping him right now, but his mind told him to leave. He was feeling nothing but hatred at the moment and didn't want to add more fuel to the fire because it wouldn't be able to be contained.

"Man, I got to get the fuck out of here." Jamison announced.

"You need me to roll with you dummy?" Tyson asked as he looked at Jamison with skeptical eyes. He knew his brother. When he wasn't good, nobody was good.

"Naw Ty I need to be alone."

"Ard dummy, don't do nothing silly." Tyson warned.

Jamison wouldn't allow anyone else to be a spectator in his turmoil. He wanted to go clear his head, alone. He and Tyson slapped hands and he nudged NuNu playfully. She threw him a quick jab to the arm and smiled. Jamison chuckled as he shook his head and made his way out.

Jamison made it to his car and before he opened his door, he placed a balled fist to the hood of his car and then rested his head there. He hated to be leaving Leah like this, he knew she wasn't okay because his heartbeat was irregular. It pumped different when she wasn't around, but he couldn't face either of them right now. Jamison opened the door to his Lexus and climbed inside. He started the engine and then sped out of the parking lot, leaving behind a trail of tire marks and the smell of burnt rubber. Faint sounds of *Mr. Ice Cream Man* by Master P were coming through his speakers. Jamison cut the music up, letting it knock through his speakers as he jumped on the highway hitting 90 miles. His mind was speeding just as fast as his car, as Stacy's words bounced around playing dodge ball in his head. He wasn't sure where he was going but he wanted to put as much distance as he could between him and the two women, he left behind in that hospital tonight.

CHAPTER 3

2 WEEKS LATER

*L*eah laid across the couch in Stacy's living room as she watched her daughter play with the new toys Marcus had sent her home with. She was grateful that Stacy was home and doing well because she was able to play the middleman between her and Marcus. Leah stared at her phone as she thought about dialing Jamison's number for the fifth time today. It had been two weeks since she seen him. Two long ass weeks since she had heard his voice, since she had felt his embrace and she desperately needed both right now. He hadn't answered the phone, hadn't responded to one single text message. Leah was confused, because though he wasn't communicating, each day she received a gift from him. Roses one day, a 3-ct tennis bracelet, envelopes filled with money, and the list goes on. He was doing all of that but wasn't talking to her and she was utterly confused. *How is he still sending me gifts, but won't talk to me?* She thought. Leah noticed Ma'Laysia putting a toy and her mouth and sat up.

"No, no Lay. What mommy say about putting toys in your mouth?"

Leah went to stop her from putting the toy in her mouth

and Ma'Laysia crawled away from her and mocked her mother.

"No, no." She said.

Leah looked at her baby girl and smiled as she shook her head.

"Just bad." She said as she scooped her up and kissed her cheek.

Leah's phone buzzed and she beelined for the couch to retrieve it.

My Nu- Are you okay boo?
Leah- No, I still haven't heard from Jamison. Me and Lay want your company.
My Nu-We will be there in 30

Leah laid her phone down before she and Ma'Laysia headed to Stacy's room to check in on her. When Leah approached her godmother's door she knocked softly before entering. Leah walked in noticing Stacy sleeping. She walked over to the bed and kissed her forehead and turned to leave until Ma'Laysia started crying and reaching for her grandma.

"Shhh, Lay. She's tired little love," Leah whispered. However, it was too late. Stacy heard her grandbaby and immediately got up. She sat up in the bed and extended her arms, reaching for her baby.

"Come on ma ma's Lay," Stacy said groggily.

"G mommy go back to sleep, I got her." Leah protested.

"Bre'Ana, give me my damn baby, shit," Stacy hissed, as she smacked her lips and rolled her eyes.

Leah smirked. She didn't know why she even tried to put up a fight because when it came to her daughter and Stacy, they were inseparable. Leah handed her daughter over and left out the room. She had enough time to jump in the shower and change out of yesterday's clothes, before NuNu and Baby Tyson arrived. She went back to the living room to fetch her phone and then headed back to her old room. Leah gathered her things for her shower as she thought of Jamison. She missed him terribly. She thought of him every day all day, hoping he was okay and praying that he would just pick up the phone and talk to her. Leah couldn't imagine the things he was going through and though she understood his disconnection, she didn't like it at all. She, in fact, hated it because she was missing her protection. Missing her shield. She still felt something for him and didn't care about Stacy being his birth mother. He was her love and she wanted him to come to her. She wanted him to tell her she wasn't crazy for still wanting him and that everything would be okay.

Leah grabbed her phone and went to his contact. *My Love.* The sight of those two words instantly gave her flutters. The day he first stored his name in her phone caused her eyes to mist. Leah knew that this was it, being with him was supposed to be her life. She clicked on his name and sent him a text. *I love and miss you.* Leah sighed as she tossed her phone back on the bed. She knew he wouldn't respond but she still wanted him to know. Wanted him to know that she still felt the same and she was truly hoping that he did too. How could he not? The chemistry they shared couldn't just be ignored. It couldn't just go away overnight. If Jamison allowed the fire of love that they had created to be put out, Leah would know it was never real.

She showered and dressed. When she entered the living room, NuNu was already there playing with her god daughter as Stacy rocked Baby Tyson to sleep. She was holding him so close and Leah noticed a tear slide down her godmother's face. She knew Stacy was thinking of the day shots had rang out at Baby Tyson's party. *Thank God, he was okay that day.*

"It's okay G mommy," Leah said in a low tone.

NuNu looked to Leah and then to Stacy. Her eyes instantly prickled as she witnessed the emotions flow from

Stacy. She placed Ma'Laysia in her lap and rubbed Stacy's back soothingly.

"It's alright ma," NuNu whispered.

Stacy wiped her face and then stood from the couch. They didn't know her thoughts. Not only did she feel bad for what happened that day while her grandkids were around, she also had her son on her mind. Jamison hadn't answered one of her phone calls and she desperately wanted to see him and explain. She wished he would just find it in his heart to listen to what she had to say and try to understand that she did what she thought would be best for him. She did what she thought was best for everyone in her life. The pain and regret that lived in her since the day she gave him up, kept Stacy up at night. Then came Leah into her life and her maternal instinct was present with her. She over loved Leah as the thoughts of the son she gave up played in her mind daily. She wondered everyday if he was okay, if he was being loved correctly. Regret filled her every single day as years passed by not knowing where he was or who he was.

"We're going to go lay down for a little while," Stacy announced before leaving the three girls to themselves.

Leah looked to NuNu with misting eyes. She was trying her best to stifle them, trying her hardest to keep them from falling. So many emotions were running through her like a stampede. Her heart went out to her god mother. She knew she was going through turmoil. Jamison had gone M.I.A in her and Stacy's life. He had completely shut them out except for when he sent gifts to Leah every day. He was a man of his word and though he had no interest in speaking to them he still kept his word.

NuNu looked at Leah with sympathy. She knew what it felt like to not have the man she loved for weeks at a time. She had experienced the same thing with Tyson. The only difference was she was able to see him when he came to get their son. Leah didn't have a baby to bond her and Jamison. There was no reason for him to contact her because there was no tiny person to keep their connection from being severed.

NuNu extended an arm out to Leah, inviting her into her space. Leah closed the space between them and laid her head on NuNu's shoulder as the tears finally broke free.

"I miss him so damn much Nuuu." She cried. Leah placed both hands to her face as she lifted slightly and began to ball. NuNu rubbed Leah's back as she bounced her god daughter who was witnessing her mother's grief. She began to fuss and NuNu stood to take her in the room with Stacy and her son. Leah remained in the same spot. She cried so hard that she began to get nauseous. She hadn't felt pain like this in a long time. What she endured with Marcus had hurt, but Jamison's absence was killing her slowly. Their chemistry was something she had never felt, and Leah felt it slowly fading as the weeks, hell as the minutes passed. She could no longer keep the contents in her stomach from spewing out of her as she rushed to the kitchen, heaving over the sink.

She lifted, as she cut the water on to rinse the sink and her mouth. NuNu walked in the kitchen and just embraced her. Neither of them said anything and in this moment, Leah was okay with that because she just needed to let this out and possibly began to move on.

Jamison laid in his king size bed, eyes to the ceiling in turmoil. The T.V. was on and the game was playing but he wasn't watching it. Jamison was lost in his thoughts. His mind was on Leah. He felt like a sucka. He was in his feelings about her when he should have been trying to get over her, but he couldn't. He could not just unlove her. He couldn't just stop wanting her. Jamison wanted Leah bad as hell. She was the one he loved. The only one he had truly loved. Since being with her, he felt complete. So, no he couldn't just shake the feeling because loving her was easy. It felt right but damn if their situation right now felt wrong. How could he still want her knowing that the woman who should have raised him gave him up and raised someone else. His heart was heavy, and mind was conflicted. Jamison read the text.

Mrs. Banks- I love and miss you.

He read the text three times before he laid his phone back on the nightstand. He tucked both hands behind his head as he stared up at the ceiling fan. Leah's message, her words ran through his mind. It was like he could hear her voice whispering the words softly in his ear. *I love and miss you.* He missed her too. He fucking loved her so much that it was sickening. Jamison hadn't been the same since finding out about his birth mother. The resentment he held towards her crippled him. He also began to grow resentment for Leah as well. He knew he shouldn't but that's how he was feeling. Resentment, love, a little hate, but then it all retracted back to love for her. Leah had got the chance to be loved and taken care of by the woman who should have been doing those very things for him. Loving him. Taking care of him. Instead, she had given him up and never looked back. Jamison began to wonder if that's why he had even fallen for her. Had she been doused in Stacy so much that it radiated off of her? Because he couldn't shake the connection that he had for Leah.

Jamison grabbed his phone again and went to Stacy's number. He didn't need to wonder how she had got his phone number. When a text message came from a number that wasn't programmed in his phone, he automatically knew it was her. He clicked on her message and reread the words.

813-622-0226
Jamison, please come talk to me. Let me explain to

*you what happened. Please don't shut me out without
at least allowing me the chance to explain. -Stacy*

Jamison read the message twice before he closed out of the messages and went to dial the number. Before he hit the green button, he paused as he allowed the dismay for her to stop him from calling her. He wanted an explanation. One was indeed owed to him, but he couldn't bring himself to face her right now. Face Leah. He closed his eyes and let out a sharp breath. He missed her terribly. His stomach tightened and a wave of nausea swept over him. Jamison stood abruptly as he rushed to the bathroom. He barely made it. The contents of his stomach flew from his mouth. Jamison couldn't remember the last time he had threw up as he continued to let everything come up. *What the fuck?* He thought. Sweat began to cover his forehead and his mind began to wonder what the hell was wrong with him. He stood, flushed the toilet and then went to the bathroom sink. Jamison stood in the mirror, staring at his reflection. He didn't know why he hadn't noticed at the hospital, but he was now seeing parts of Stacy within him. He shook his head as he cut the water on splashing his face and then put water in his mouth to remove the residue.

Jamison heard his doorbell ring and finished gathering himself before exiting the bathroom. He sauntered down the long hallway and then descended the stairs as whoever was at the door pushed the doorbell again. He didn't even look to see who it was he was so out of it. When he pulled the door open, there stood Chels.

"JJ, please talk to me," Chels pleaded.

Jamison shook his head and then slammed the door in her face. He heard her yelling through the door but didn't care what she was talking about. Stacy and Leah were on his mind heavy and he wanted to go to them. He made his way to the kitchen and grabbed a bottle of Hennessy out of his liquor cabinet. He needed the brown liquid to dull the pain a little bit. Chels was still banging and knocking at his door but he was unmoved. Jamison didn't have time for her shit. He didn't even know why the hell she was even on his doorstep. He retrieved his burner phone from the kitchen island and dialed Tyson's number. His brother's presence was much wanted right now because Jamison was beginning to lose his mind.

Jamison grabbed his keys, the Hennessy, slid into some Retro Jordan's and headed out the front door. He was going to meet Tyson at the club. Chels stood on the porch and Jamison walked right by her.

"JJ, talk to me please. I love you and I'm sorry." She called out.

Jamison stopped and turned around. He laid burning red eyes on her and shook his head. *She just can't let go*, he thought.

"Chels go home. We're done. Go bug your baby daddy with ya boppin' ass."

Chels scoffed. She walked off the porch and stood in front of him.

"So, you're just going to throw away years with me. Just like that."

"Just like that." Jamison said with a snap of his fingers.

"Now leave before I go put a restraining order on your ass." He said walking off.

Jamison climbed in his car and pulled off. He wasn't into wasting any more time with his past when his future was crying out for him. He was going to talk to his brother. He needed Tyson to give him advice on what to do because right now his mind was kicking his hearts ass in the war they were fighting.

CHAPTER 4

*M*arcus cruised the city with his homie City riding shotgun, and Shan Shan in the back seat of his Regal sitting on 22-inch rims. His original riders before him and Tyson became close, but now that friendship was over. With Spring being right around the corner, the weather had everyone in the city out. Marcus switched in and out of the lanes, wanting to be seen, as *Wanksta* by 50 Cent blared through his speakers. Marcus had been going full throttle in the streets. When he didn't have his daughter, nothing but money was on his mind. He and his boys stayed hitting licks, becoming the stick-up kids of the city. Getting it, making a real come up. The boys pulled up to City Park where a city-wide basketball game was being held. There were teams from each high school in the city set up to play in the tournament. When the boys pulled up all eyes were on them. The girls from the south side flocked to Marcus's car when they noticed City and Shan Shan climbing out. They were them boys on their side of town. Getting to the money and chasing the hoods boppers, just like old times before Leah came in and captured Marcus's heart. Marcus climbed out the car after his boys. He scanned the scene as he watched girls approach his boys. The south side girls did something to him. They had a different swag about them which had made him attracted to Leah. This was her side of town, but she was the only one that truly stood out to him. Being in her area made him want to pull up at Stacy's house just to see if she was there. Leah had been a ghost in his world. She never answered his phone calls, never responded to a text. He was sure that she had built her wall so damn high that she, herself wouldn't be able to climb down. He shook his head as he thought of her, he had fucked up and now she was letting the next nigga get what was supposed to be his.

"Marc, nigga get out of yo head," City said, snapping Marcus out of his thoughts.

"Nigga you good?" Shan Shan asked.

Marcus nodded.

"Well let's go watch these little nigga's play then and get some bets going." Shan Shan stated.

The trio walked over to the court where the game was taking place. They slapped hands with different boys from around the hood and gave a few head nods to others that wasn't from the south. They placed bets on some of the little young boys that attended the high schools they were from. The true rivalry was Libbey and Scott always. Everyone in the city attended just to watch those two schools. Marcus being from the North side of Toledo put his money on his home school, while City and Shan Shan placed bets on the best to do it. They were Cowboys and rode out for their school, always. The high school boys were ripping the court up, putting down their game. The crowd was going crazy as they watched the two schools battle it out. Marcus looked across the court and spotted Leah standing next to NuNu. His heart sank at the sight of his daughter's mother. She was beautiful, wearing a grey and black sweatsuit with those damn Jordan's she loved on her feet to match. He was taking a back for a moment as if it was his first time seeing her. Marcus rubbed a hand down his wavy head as he stared at her from across the court. The sound of his ringing phone was the only thing able to get him to take his eyes off her. He looked down at the phone not recognizing the number. *Who the fuck is this?* He thought. Normally he didn't answer numbers he didn't know, but something was telling him to answer this call.

"Hello," Marcus answered as he began to walk in the direction of his car.

Chrissy was on the other end. She was screaming and yelling. It was time. Her and Marcus' son was getting ready to be born and she needed him to get to her. Marcus' mind began to spin. The realization that he was getting ready to have a child outside of Leah became clearer than ever.

"I'm… I'm on my way." He said fumbling over his words.

Marcus ran back to where his homies were standing.

"Yo, I'm out Chrissy having the baby." Marcus announced as he slapped hands with each of them.

They got loud as they yelled congratulations. They were going to celebrate later, but first Marcus had to get to the hospital to see his son make an entrance. He didn't get a chance to see his daughter born and was excited to witness his son being born. Marcus looked to Leah and this time they locked eyes. A look of disgust spread across her face, causing her smile to fade instantly. Marcus shook his head as he watched her move through the crowd pulling NuNu with her. *Damn,* he thought. It was truly as if they were now strangers, sharing a child that one wouldn't have thought they created out of love at one point in time.

"I'm out." Marcus said as he slapped hands with his squad again. He had already stayed around longer than he should have, knowing he didn't want to miss the birth of his son. Marcus rushed to his car and sped out of the parking lot, kicking up dust as his tires spun trying to grip the pavement.

∿

NuNu and Leah began to walk back towards Stacy's house. Seeing Marcus had put Leah in a mood, and she didn't care to stay at the park any longer. She had been doing good at avoiding him, having Stacy as the middleman. The moment they locked eyes Leah had caught an instant attitude. He was the last person she expected to see at the park. The type of resentment Leah had built up with Marcus was unhealthy. She loved her daughter with every fiber in her bones but who she created her with, she felt nothing but hatred for. He had taken her through hell in less than a year. Who she thought was her knight in shining armor, turned out to be her world that never rotated on its axis. He kept her cloaked in darkness. It was times like this when she would need Jamison. He was always able to settle her and erase ill feelings with just his presence. However, it felt as if he had taken his love away. Snatched it right back from her, without warning. *Fucking Indian giver.* Where was he when she needed him? It had been weeks and he still wasn't reaching back out.

"Leah boo, you okay?" NuNu asked as they walked up on Stacy's porch taking a seat on the steps.

Leah shook her head. She wasn't okay. She missed Jamison like crazy. Leah was missing her man and that fucking monster that scared the best orgasms out of her. He had loved her good and then life shifted in a direction, no one expected, causing them to pull apart involuntarily.

"Have you seen Jamison?" she asked in a low tone.

"He still hasn't answered me or g mommy."

NuNu shook her head. She hadn't seen him. Tyson barely heard from him and when he did it was always short and about business at the club. NuNu didn't know that Tyson had just met up with Jamison. He hadn't divulged the information to her. She felt bad seeing melancholy all over her best friend. NuNu knew how much Leah loved Jamison. Shit, she knew how much he loved her as well. She felt her hurt but she also knew that Jamison was on the worst end of the situation. She felt the most sorrow for him. He was a man that was adopted and even though his parents loved him wholeheartedly, he was still wanting to know his birth mother. He still wanted to know why she had given him up. Had Stacy not raised Leah as her own, then maybe the situation would be different right now. However, she had raised someone as her own and the realization had hurt him to his core.

"Nu, I miss him," Leah cried as she laid her head on NuNu's shoulder. NuNu pulled Leah into her, embracing her tightly.

"Don't cry boo." She whispered.

"It'll be okay. That boy loves you too much to stay away for too long. Just give him time. He deserves that time. I can only imagine how he's feeling right now Leah."

Leah nodded. She knew NuNu was right, it didn't make knowing she was right hurt any less though. She wanted her shield. She wanted to feel his love and his touch because it was the best feeling in the world outside of having her daughter. A wave of nausea swept over. *I shouldn't have eaten them damn hot dogs*, she thought.

"I'm about to be sick," she said as she gagged slightly. Leah stood and raced in the house. NuNu stood as she shook her head. Right away Lena's words played in NuNu's mind. *By the looks of it, you look pregnant bitch.* Her eyes widened and instantly misted. "Leah ass pregnant," she whispered.

NuNu rushed in the house. Stacy looked up from the couch in alarm.

"What the hell is wrong?" She quizzed.

"Nothing, g mommy. She saw Marcus and she's just upset now." NuNu said telling half of the truth.

NuNu made her way into the bathroom, where Leah was now rinsing her mouth out. She closed the door quickly behind her and stared at Leah. Studying her close, trying to see if she could see the signs of pregnancy on her. Leah looked at her confused.

"Nu, what you are staring at, heffa?"

"Leah, you pregnant?" NuNu asked.

NuNu didn't hesitate, she didn't even try to beat around the bush. This was the second time she had witnessed Leah get sick within a week. So, she was now beginning to wonder if Lena's words could actually hold some truth to it. Even though she was a shitty mother, she was still a mother and they always knew things like that.

Leah looked at NuNu as if she were crazy. *Is she fucking serious?* She cocked her head back and then thought of Lena's words as well and shook her head.

"Nu'Asia don't let my damn egg donor make you start believing that shit, cause I'm not pregnant. I'm on the Depo shot and that shit is almost impossible." She said snappishly.

NuNu sighed in relief.

"Okay, I'm just making sure boo. Yo ass been sick twice already since she said that."

Leah shook her head.

"Yeah, sick because I'm having monster withdrawals and shit." She said laughing.

The girls burst out into laughter. Leah knew she wasn't pregnant. She kicked herself because she knew she shouldn't have eaten them nasty ass hotdogs they were serving at the park. Her stomach wasn't right since she consumed them. NuNu shook her head as she opened the bathroom door so they could make their way back into the living room where Stacy was with their children.

"Everything okay?" Stacy asked as she looked up at the girls who were giggling when they entered the room.

"Yeah," They both said in unison.

"Jinx," They said again in unison.

They all shared a laughed. Stacy smiled as she watched

the girls. They were her girls, her babies, who now had babies. Her mind drifted to Jamison. She hoped he was okay and wished that he would talk to her. Stacy knew that a conversation between him and Leah also needed to be had as well and prayed that they would talk soon as well.

CHAPTER 5

ONE WEEK LATER

*D*ominic sat, head spinning from the liquor as images of Mandy flashed in his mind. She was beautiful. The night they had been downtown in a hotel looking at the city's skyline was on constant repeat. She had posed for him for three hours as he sketched her, one of the best nights of his life. A small smile spread across his face and then disappeared because now she was gone. Again. He knew they had done something to her. He was certain. That's why he took it upon himself to wait for the perfect time to try his best to eliminate everyone he thought was involved. His main target was Leah. It was because of her that any of this was even taking place. Had she just minded her business and let the beef cool down none of this would have happened.

Dominic sat cloaked in darkness, in the middle of the day. He was uncomfortable and was sipping in hot air. He heard doors clang open and began bucking against the ropes that held him in place. The ropes were so tight that it tore through his skin from pulling so hard. Tyson and Jamison made their way to where he was tied up and stared at him. They looked at each other then, Jamison removed the pillowcase from his head. Dominic immediately hawked up his saliva and spit in Jamison's face.

"Fuck you, you soft ass nigga," Dominic said with malice.

Jamison grimaced as he swiped a hand down his face. *No, the fuck he didn't,* he thought. Jamison punched him so hard, that he knocked his two front teeth out and sent him crashing to the dirty cement. They were in an old warehouse that he and Tyson's stepdad had owned. He handed it over to the boys once they were older and they used it to hide their product. Now they were using it for more than just that. Dominic had disrespected by shooting up Tyson's son's party. He took that very personal.

Jamison came up off his hip and pointed the Glock 43 right in the middle of Dominic's forehead as he laid on his back.

"You bitch ass nigga."

Tyson stepped up and grabbed his brother.

"JJ, no dummy," Tyson said in his heavy Baltimore accent. "Stick to the plan."

"Fuck y'all!" Dominic yelled.

"Just know something happen to me and I bet my peoples pay y'all a visit."

Jamison looked to Tyson and then back to Dominic. He lifted slowly and then turned the pistol around and sent the butt of the gun crashing into Dominic's nose. Splitting it instantly.

"Shut the fuck up pussy." He said as he lifted his black Timberland and kicked him in the face.

Tyson lifted Dominic from the pavement and stood in front of him, arms folded and anger flaring. The nigga was so hot that his light skin was a deep red. He dismissed the threat Dominic had just made. Tyson would always be ready for whoever, whenever. Dominic had put his entire family in danger and went ghost for two weeks. That was until Jamison forced the nigga Mont to tell them where he was at. Dominic could have easily taken his family from him and that sent Tyson through the roof at just the thought. He sent his fist across Dominic's jaw, collapsing it as soon as his fist connected.

"You almost took my son, clown ass nigga. You shot up my world's shit, put him and everyone I love in danger dummy, and for that, you owe!" He barked. Tyson was so angry that he spit while he talked, and his accent was heavy.

Dominic couldn't speak, he just groaned in agony as his head hung low. He tried to spit and couldn't do that, blood just dripped from his mouth. Tyson wasn't the one to act with so much aggression and rage, but Dominic had crossed the line. He had crossed the nigga that grew up in the streets of Baltimore. The nigga that was labeled as soft because of his looks but was the most dangerous when provoked. No one saw that side of him, he kept that nigga tucked away. His uncle had taught him self-control. He had taught him when to turn on the dangerous side. That clap on and clap off type shit and now was the time Tyson was clapping that shit on.

Tyson pulled his burner from his back and Jamison handed him the silencer. Though they were in an empty warehouse and it was the middle of the day, and no one was out, they wanted to be cautious. He aimed for the middle of Dominic's forehead and took a deep breath. Tyson had never wanted to be this type of man, but Dominic had disrespected. He had almost lost his son because of him and Tyson was going to solve the problem one way and one way only.

"You got anything to say, before you go rest at the bottom of the swamp next to your bitch, nigga?" Jamison asked as he smirked.

Dominic's eyes widened. *Mandy*, he thought. His head hung low and he groaned as tears fell. This was it. He was finally about to be with his love and their son. He hadn't thought it would come around on him so soon. He didn't know how they had even caught up to him because no one knew about his where abouts except Mont. *Damn*, he thought. Mont had ratted him out. His best friend had turned on him, giving up his location. It was clear that Mont was playing both sides and that hurt Dominic deep. He gathered all the strength he had to speak.

"Mont fucked your bitch you pretty muthafucka! That's his shorty she's carrying nigga," Dominic said before turning to Tyson. Jamison punched him before he could say anything else. Dominic groaned as pain shot throughout his entire body.

"Fuck you, nigga." Jamison shot back.

Tyson sat Dominic up straight and aimed the pistol right back to his head. Dominic's eyes were closed but he still managed to say his last words before Tyson let off four shots to his dome.

"I fucked NuNu pretty ass."

Those words sent Tyson over the edge. He saw nothing but red as he let off shot after shot. They left Dominic sitting in the chair slumped, brains everywhere. *I fucked NuNu pretty ass. I fucked NuNu pretty ass.* It was on a constant repeat in Tyson's mind as he and Jamison made their exit.

"I'll pay someone to come dump the nigga in the swamp, he can rest peacefully at the bottom with his bitch." Jamison said.

Tyson shook his head and gave his brother a smirk. However, he was pissed. He never had a nigga disrespect him by claiming to fuck his lady. Tyson had never been the one to be an insecure nigga, but the statement had him bothered.

"Ty," Jamison called out, snapping Tyson out of his thoughts.

"What's good dummy?" Tyson shot back as they made their way to their cars.

"Don't forget we got shit to handle at the club tonight, make sure you meet me there on time."

Tyson nodded and hopped in his car. He reached for his

ringing phone and looked down at it shocked. Leah's name appeared on the screen and he answered immediately. He held a finger up to Jamison, who was yelling his name. Tyson listened to Leah as she cried and talked.

"Ok lor boss, I got you," Tyson said before hanging up the phone.

He looked to Jamison and shook his head. He knew the situation was heavy, but he still didn't like the fact that Jamison had not contacted Leah in three weeks. Now she was on his line asking him to talk to his brother and hearing her cry pissed Tyson off even more.

"Yo, don't you think it's time to talk to Leah and Stacy, if not your mom at least my fucking sister dummy. Got her calling me crying and shit. I told you how to handle it and yo dumb ass still ain't handled it."

Jamison shook his head, trying his hardest to fight back emotions. He hadn't thought about his current situation and now he was feeling fucked up all over again. To hear that Leah was crying over him had him kicking himself on the inside. He missed the hell out of her, but how was he supposed to be with her after finding out his mother raised her. He couldn't be with her after that, even though he wanted to. Jamison had never loved anyone the way that he loved Leah. She was his rib and to have to let her go was killing him.

"It's on Ty," Jamison replied simply before pulling off.

Tyson pulled up to his home and killed the engine. His family had been in harm's way and it hadn't sat well with him since that day. He felt like he was starting to lose control over things but quickly shook the thought. The only threats had been eliminated. Now he could go in here to his family and put today's events behind him. Tyson climbed out the car, letting the cool breeze hit his face. It was a beautiful day, as Spring began to creep in slowly.

Fuck it I'm about to take lor Ty to the park today, he thought as he made his way up to the front door. Tyson opened the door and his son noticed him immediately. He dropped his toy car and put hurried little feet to the hardwood floors to get to his daddy. Tyson dropped his keys and ran in place with his arms opened wide, waiting to receive his son. Baby Tyson was smiling as he ran into his daddy.

"Da, da, da, da,"

Tyson smiled as he lifted his son in the air.

"What's good my world?" Tyson said as he tossed his baby in the air slightly.

There was no denying the love he had for his son. When he looked at Baby Tyson all he saw was a mini version of himself. The fact that he could have been gone at the hands of Dominic caused him to grow angry for a moment. Tyson didn't know what he would have done had that turned out differently. It made him begin to cherish his son and lady that much more.

NuNu watched the father and son moment as she laid on the couch watching *BAPS* on BET. She would never get used to seeing the sight, it would always be like the first time she gave birth, and the way Tyson held their son afterwards touch her in a way that she had never been. Their bond was everything and she would always be grateful for the man who she knew she was made for. She sat up, once the boys made their way over to her, taking a seat right next to her. She looked at Tyson and could tell something was bothering him. NuNu knew her man well. She knew something was wrong, it was etched all in his face.

"What's wrong baby?" she asked as she leaned into him, resting her head on his shoulder.

Tyson looked down at her and sighed. He paused for a beat before answering her. Dominic's words played with his mind. He didn't know why but a what if lived in his mind after that. NuNu had told him she was a virgin when they first met. He knew that to be true but then he was away a few times and he had left home for weeks. However, he wanted to trust his lady, she had never shown him anything different outside of what he already knew.

"I got a question," he said, kissing the top of her head. The scent of melon shampoo met his nostrils and he inhaled it one more time before he finished speaking.

"Would you ever fuck around on me Lor Mama?"

NuNu lifted as confusion spread through her. Her eyes squinted and she stared at him for a moment. *Is this nigga fucking serious?*

"Ty, I'd never play you like that. I'm a firm believer in do unto others as you would want done unto you."

Tyson kissed her nose and then her lips. Her answer was solid, and he believed every word. She was his lor mama, so he knew she'd never cross that line. Tyson knew he was tripping. He knew he shouldn't have asked, but he had to in order to slow down his racing mind. NuNu's face was still twisted up from the question and he knew he had to disarm her before it went any further.

"Fix your face Lor Mama."

"Naw, why the hell you ask me that out of nowhere?" She quizzed in irritation.

Tyson shook his head and knew he needed to move quickly.

"Nu'Asia go lay the baby down and then come back down here and let me bend that lor shit over."

Tyson leaned in and stuck his tongue in her mouth. Just like that NuNu melted into him, giving in. She was soft when it came to him. She would never be able to turn him down once he said her first name and some nasty shit in the same sentence. It made her wet instantly. Always. She moaned as she bit into his bottom lip softly.

"I'm going to let the shit slide cause, you got me ready to get hit," she said with a smirk.

Tyson shook his head and laughed. He should have known she would have something slick to say. It never failed. He handed her their son, and she ascended the stairs to go lay him down for his nap. When NuNu returned, Tyson was sitting on the couch awaiting her with nothing but his boxers on. NuNu walked over to him slowly as she removed pieces of her clothing one by one. She was anticipating him the whole time she was upstairs putting their son to sleep. She stood in front of him completely naked, staring as he stared up at her. Lust filled both of their eyes and a sexy smirk crossed Tyson's face. He pulled his throbbing man from his boxers and allowed it to swing back and forth, hypnotizing her. NuNu's mouth watered and her clit pulsed as she stared down at him. Tyson stroked himself as NuNu watched in anticipation. The way Tyson had her squirming where she stood, he knew she was ready. He could see the silky moisture seeping between her southern lips.

"Time to bend that lor shit over lor mama."

Tyson bit into his bottom lip and NuNu hopped on him.

CHAPTER 6

*J*amison pulled up to Stacy's house relieved that Leah's car wasn't sitting outside. He wouldn't be able to handle both of them in one sitting. He could, but he wouldn't. It would all be too much to deal with at once. The conversation with Stacy is one he wanted to do with only them in the room. He killed the engine to his 72 droptop Cutlass. The same car he had Leah hoisted on his dashboard in, in the middle of winter. Memories of that night danced in his mental and he bit down into his bottom lip as he visualized the way she slid up and down on his pole. He quickly shook the image from his head when he noticed Stacy come from off the porch.

He climbed out of the car and approached her slowly. Stacy gave him a half smile as she took him in. She took the time to study him before she spoke. Looking at his tall frame. Studying the way his forehead crinkled, a trait that he got from her because she crinkled hers the same way. His eyes were hers as well. He was handsome. Her handsome son, and she couldn't help but allow the corners of her mouth to turn up more.

"Should we walk while we talk, or do you prefer that we sit?"

Jamison shrugged. It really didn't matter to him what they did. He was just ready to get this over with. He was tired of running. Tired of dodging phone calls. A lecture from the father who had raised him forced him to man up and finally face the inevitable.

"Okay, let's sit." She said.

Stacy walked back up her walkway, taking a seat on the step. She looked at her hands and dusted them off as she waited for Jamison to have a seat. When he finally filled the space next to her, she let out a sharp breath. This was it. It was time to face her past. They both sat silent. Muted, not really wanting to press play on the story that was about to be told. Neither of them, were ready for how it would begin or end. When Stacy laid eyes on Jamison they misted, betraying her in that moment. She knew she owed him so much and it hurt her to her heart to know that she had caused him pain. Stacy knew that she needed to hurry up and start explaining. The look on Jamison's face let her know that he was tired of waiting. So, she did it. She was finally about to press play on the story that she didn't think she would ever have to tell again.

"Jamison, I hope you fully understand what I am about to tell you and find it in your heart to forgive me after it's all said."

She paused as she swiped her hand through her short hair, stopping at her neck as she let out a sigh. Jamison could see signs of remorse. He could feel it even, that's how connected he felt to her. He knew it was about to get deep. Something was telling him to get up and just say all was forgiven but another part of him begged him to hear what he knew he was owed.

"I wasn't ready to be a mother. I wasn't fit to be your mother," Stacy said as a tear slid down her face. She sniffed and quickly swiped it away as she let her mind tell the story of her past.

Stacy entered the house from her junior high school's football game, dressed in her blue and silver cheerleading outfit. Her long hair was pulled into a ponytail with spiraled silver ribbons dangling from it. She tossed her cheer bag in the corner by the front door as she made her way through the living room. The house was empty as she made her way to her bedroom. Her mother must had been mandated at work because she normally was home by 8pm every evening. Stacy did her normal as she came out of her clothes once she entered her bedroom so that she could take her nightly shower before bed.

Stacy emerged from the bathroom with a towel wrapped snuggly around her, after her shower. She was startled to see her mother's boyfriend as he stepped out of their bedroom.

"Hey Face," she said as she proceeded to her bedroom.

He gave her a nod and then continued his conversation on the phone as he swaggered to the front room. Stacy entered her room, turned her radio on and danced around her room as she got dressed. When she was done, she grabbed her History book out of her bookbag and made her way to the bed so that she could do some late cramming before her test the next morning. Before she knew it, she had dozed off and was being awakened out of her sleep to the feeling of her bottoms being removed. She looked down to see Face between her legs. She tried to scramble against her headboard, but he hurriedly hovered over her and covered her mouth before she could scream. Tears immediately slid down her face as she stared at his eyes. They were bloodshot red and white residue was on his nose. He was high. Stacy could tell and when he was high, he was never himself. Terror set in her bones as she wondered where her mother was. Face spread her legs and broke the seal to her innocence. Stacy laid there in silence as silent tears fell while she listened to the ticks of the clock on her wall. Three hundred and twenty-one ticks passed before he finished. He kissed the side of her cheek.

"You say anything, it'll be the last thing you utter." He whispered as he climbed off her, leaving his DNA behind.

He departed from her bedroom and Stacy let out a gut-wrenching cry. She hurriedly covered her mouth with both hands as her emotions spilled down her face. She was in pain down there. Where was her mother? Hours had passed before she heard her. Stacy was too fearful to even move. She listened as she heard her mother and Face have sex that night and the contents of her stomach erupted from her. He was sick. He had just violated her and now was in the next room sexing her mother.

The sun's rays kissed Stacy's face as she stared at the ceiling. Sleep never came as she laid in bed with puffy eyes from crying all night. Her body wasn't mobile until she heard Face leaving for work that morning. She rushed to the shower, allowing the water to be as hot as she could stand it and scrubbed. Scrubbed until she was red and raw. Her cries could be heard from the bathroom and her mother entered.

"Stephanie. What's wrong?"

Stacy quickly snatched her towel from the shower pole and covered her body as she rushed to her mother. Her words were trapped in her throat as she sobbed and then Face's words echoed in her ear causing her to shiver. Instant terror. She couldn't say anything, she wouldn't. Would her mother even believe her? Stacy didn't want to risk it, so she opted for silence and forced out a quick lie.

9 months later

Stacy screamed. She felt her bones cracking as she struggled to give birth to a baby boy. No one knew that she was giving birth to her mother's boyfriend's baby. Stacy had told her mother that she had had sex one time with a boy that she had known from school but had moved away. She still didn't have the courage to tell her mother the truth out of fear. She was 14 years old giving birth to a little boy that she wouldn't be keeping. She and her mother decided that it would be in the best interest of this baby to go to a deserving family and that could provide a suitable life for him. Stacy's heart ached knowing that she would be giving up her baby. She cried as her son passed through the birth canal, splitting her opening as she birthed him. Her heart melted at the sound of his cries and though she knew she wasn't going to keep him, she still wanted to lay eyes on him. The doctor placed her son on her chest and the spark that Stacy felt caused her eyes to mist instantly. There was an instant connection she felt as soon as his little body touched hers.

She kissed the top of his head. Her mother stepped up and rubbed the top of Stacy's head as she witnessed her daughter's turmoil.

"I love you and I am so sorry. You will be the only one to ever know what my heart sounds like from the inside, because I will never have another." Stacy whispered as she cried right before her baby boy was lifted from her chest. She had just made her only child a promise to never have another because she knew she was robbing him of the chance to be raised by the woman who had birthed him. She didn't even want to name him, she felt it would be too disrespectful to do so, knowing that she was giving him away.

Jamison listened as Stacy told her story. Her voice was soft and held hurt. Most of all it held remorse from the decision she had made. His heart was beating out of his chest as the hatred he had once harbored instantly turned into love. He understood why she did what she felt was right. He couldn't say he agreed fully, but he did understand. Jamison felt remorse of his own knowing that he was a product of a rapist. He was sick to his stomach knowing that she had endured such torture and he was the now the living outcome.

Jamison stood and pulled Stacy into him. She crumbled instantly in his arms.

"I'm sorry Jamison," she cried

"I'm so damn sorry."

Jamison couldn't control his emotions as he cried with her.

"It's okay, I understand." He whispered as they rocked back and forth.

"Thank you for telling me, and as selfish as this may sound, thank you for keeping your promise to me. That makes this a little easier to swallow, knowing that you kept that promise after all these years.

Stacy pulled back and looked up at him. She couldn't believe that this was her baby. The life that she had let go of. She shook her head as more regret filled her. Stacy's mind began to race as she thought of how she should have just kept him. She could have figured everything out along the way but then she wouldn't have been too sure if he would have turned out to be the same man that he was today standing in front of her.

"I couldn't break that, once it was spoken it was a mandatory law that I had written and signed off on."

Jamison swiped his nose and nodded.

"Where do we go from here?" he asked.

Stacy smiled.

"Well I would love to get to know you, but first I think it's some things between you and Leah that needs to be worked out. She loves you and I'm certain that you love her. So, you two need to figure this out and then we all can go from there. I don't want any more time between you two to be wasted by my past mistakes."

"I don't know how me and her can ever be together if your…"

Stacy shook her head and cut him off.

"The love you two share has nothing to do with me," she said smiling.

"She's not your real sister Jamison. It's okay to love her."

"I love her so fucking much. I miss her like hell, man." Jamison said.

Tears slid down his face. The love he had for Leah was palpable. Stacy wiped his face and then grabbed him by the head. She stared at him for a beat. She was staring into the face of a man. A man that she knew was going to be the one to love her daughter perfectly. Their situation was a complicated one but that didn't mean that they should give up on the love that was destined for them. Their paths were crossed for a reason and Stacy was a firm believer in everything happens for a reason.

"It's O… K… Jamison. Go to her," she said.

Jamison nodded. Stacy was right. It was inevitable. There was no sense in trying to fight the temptation. He had found real love in Leah. He had come across the best woman to love because the one before her just wasn't it. Jamison didn't want to let the connection be severed. Leah was his and he was hers. Their short encounter had caused them to create a love so pure that even their crazy reality wouldn't be able to taint it. It was time for him to go get his sweetie. He had been away from her for too long. He needed her and he was certain that she needed him because even though he was absent he could still sense her need for him. She was calling out for him every night and every day and he had been ignoring her calls. Jamison had been turning a cheek to her need for him and was feeling fucked up about it.

"What if she doesn't want this no more?" he asked.

Stacy smacked her lips and put a hand on her hip. He was crazy to even let that slip out of his mouth. Jamison grinned and shrugged his shoulders.

"Mmhmm," Stacy said with a grin of her own.

"You know damn well that girl wants you. Now stop all this stuntin' you doing and call that girl."

Jamison pulled Stacy in for another hug. He squeezed her tight and then released her. Stacy pulled back and then kissed his cheek. She put a hand to the place she left a kiss and held his face. *Life works in mysterious ways*, she thought as she stared up at him.

"Everything is going to be just fine." She whispered.

CHAPTER 7

*L*eah sat in NuNu's living room playing on her Myspace page. It was the newest thing to hit the internet. A form of social media, where you could connect with whoever. Leah was adding all type of nigga's, making her page pop with different music that would play when people came across her page, as she waited for NuNu to finish dinner. She scrolled her page as she came across Chrissy myspace on her suggested friend's list. *This bitch*. Leah rolled her eyes but couldn't help but click on her page. The first thing she saw was a picture of Chrissy in a hospital bed holding a newborn. Leah's heart sank at the sight. *She had that fucking baby*. She thought as she scrolled further down the page.

"Nu, bitch come here really quick!" She yelled.

When Leah came across the picture of Marcus holding his son, she died on the inside. Her eyes misted automatically, and it felt like her heart was being ripped into a million and one pieces. She didn't want Marcus. They were past that point, well at least she was but she couldn't help feeling hurt on the inside. She was staring at an image that should have never been her reality. He was sitting there holding a mini him. A mini him that at one point in time should have been a mini them. However, he had let another chick swoop in and snatch her family. *Damn, this nigga really had another baby outside of our daughter.* A tear slid down her face and she quickly swiped it away as she continued to stare at the picture. NuNu emerged from the kitchen with a plate in her hand.

"What is it boo?" she asked as she set the plate at the computer desk next to Leah.

Leah quickly sniffed away her emotions, there was no sense in being hurt or mad. They were past the point of returning back to what could have been. The moment Leah found out Chrissy was pregnant, she was done. As soon as she thought of giving him another chance, the thought was erased immediately. Leah would never be able to handle being with him again after that. The girl had always been around. She had whooped Chrissy's ass and went in her pockets at the club but yet she stuck around being something temporary until he made her permanent.

"Bitch, look at Marcus and Chrissy baby," she said pointing at the screen.

NuNu took a seat next to Leah and looked at the monitor. Her face twisted up in disgust as she looked at the picture of Marcus holding his son. She shook her head, NuNu couldn't stand him and was beyond glad that he and Leah were threw.

"Girl, that baby ugly ass fuck." NuNu said shaking her head.

Leah looked at her and burst into laughter. NuNu's ass never sugar coated a damn thing, and she wouldn't start now. She called it like she saw it.

"Nu, be nice damn."

"Shit that was me being nice. I could have said much worse." NuNu shot back.

Leah laughed as she continued to go through the pictures. She came across the baby's hospital preview pictures and paused as she read the name underneath the picture. *MarKest DaShan Hill.* She shook her head. *This nigga named this fucking baby what was supposed to be our son's name,* she thought. Leah didn't know why, but she was somewhat jealous. Chrissy had given him the one thing that only she was supposed to. However, just as quick as the spark of jealousy crept through her, it disappeared. Leah snapped out of it realizing that at the end of the day, she was better off without Marcus and he never would have deserved to have another child with her.

NuNu looked at Leah and saw the makings of sadness. She didn't want Leah dwelling on the past so she quickly took her mind off what should have not been.

"No, boo. Don't even get to acting salty. Fuck that nigga and his ugly ass baby and that baby ugly ass mama, with her dirty ass."

Leah looked at NuNu with shocked eyes. One thing NuNu was, was well aware of when it was something wrong with her best friend.

"Matter of fact. Let me see that damn keyboard."

NuNu clicked on the picture and scanned the comments as people were all congratulating Chrissy on her new bundle of joy. She smirked and shook her head at all the comments of how cute the baby was. *Now, why the fuck is they lying to this hoe.* She didn't like Chrissy. Never had since the day she and Leah had rolled up on her and Marcus at the night club. NuNu began to type. She felt Leah staring and smiled. NuNu knew she was petty, even childish for what she was about to do but she could care less.

"Nu, what the hell you about to say?" Leah asked.

This baby ain't even fresh out the pussy no more and still looks like a fucking senior citizen. Ugly ass little boy. The one and only NuNu.

CLICK.

"Nu'Asia!" Leah yelled as she laughed and tried to delete the comment. NuNu snatched the keyboard back from her.

"Your ass is a mess."

NuNu shrugged. She didn't care about nothing or no one that wasn't family. She knew she was wrong, but it wasn't Leah's baby with Marcus, so it didn't matter to her. NuNu peered at the screen and saw a reply.

Who the fuck talks about people kids??? A miserable bitch whose friend got their baby daddy snatched, that's who. But keep my son out of this or the problems you're seeking, I will help you find.

"Oh, this bitch talking that talk," NuNu said as her fingers went to work. She was all over Chrissy's response as Leah geeked her up the entire time.

Tyson descended the steps and shook his head as he approached the girls.

"Lor Mama!" He called out, startling them both.

He had just hung up the phone with Marcus. Chrissy had called him as soon as she saw the comment about their son. Marcus knew NuNu was savage, but he didn't think she'd stoop so low and talk about his son. He also didn't want the beef, so he thought he'd say something to Tyson hoping that he would get his lady in line. Tyson saw the plate on the computer desk and shook his head. He was going to address the issue with the baby, but first thing was first. He needed to know why the hell; he didn't have a plate waiting for him.

"Nu'Asia, that better be my plate that's sitting there," he said in a stern tone.

Shit. NuNu thought. She knew she better be quick on her toes if she didn't want there to be issues with him.

"Yes, baby." She lied.

Tyson smirked. *Her little lying ass.* He knew she was lying, but he wasn't about to press the issue. He grabbed the plate and began to eat as he took a seat on the couch.

"Why you down here talking about people kids, lor mama?"

NuNu smirked. She didn't know why he acted like this was something new with her. She said whatever was on her mind.

No one was safe not even a newborn. NuNu put her hand on her hip and cocked her head to the side.

"Ty, look at that fucking baby," she said as she pointed to the screen.

"It ain't my fault the little muthafucka qualify for his retirement plan already."

Tyson and Leah both looked at each other and shook their heads as they laughed.

"What is wrong with your baby mama Ty?" Leah asked.

Tyson dug back into his plate. He knew exactly what was wrong with her. *Her ass crazy*, he thought but opted to keep the thought to himself. He simply shook his head and smirked. NuNu was his everything. They were opposite but as they say, opposites attract. He was the positive, she was the negative, that were pulled together. She was for him and he was for her. That's just how it was. They just fit. Tyson looked over to NuNu and smiled. *My lor mama.* He was always mesmerized by her beauty. He thought back to the first day he saw her down in Florida. Tyson shook his head as he bit into his bottom lip. *Her and that orange swimsuit*, he thought. He stood, making his way over to her and kissed her lips as he sat the plate down next to her. Tyson pulled her up from the computer chair and put her over his shoulders.

NuNu yelped in surprise.

"Ty," she said as he began to carry her towards the stairs.

"What are you doing?"

Tyson didn't answer her. Instead, he turned to Leah.

"Let yourself out boss, she about to be busy for the rest of the night."

With that, he continued up the stairs. Leah and NuNu both looked at each other with shocked eyes as NuNu's panties instantly became wet. *This nigga*, she thought as she shook her head. Tyson was about to lay her body down right and she knew it. She didn't know where the certain urge had come from, but she was with it. She was always with it. Shit, she wanted it just as much as he did and was about to give it all to him. NuNu never had an issue with wanting to keep her man satisfied and tonight would be no different, even if that meant Leah would be letting herself out. When Tyson's manhood called NuNu answered that shit on the first ring never allowing it to ring twice.

Leah pulled up to Stacy's and the car in front of her came as a shock. She hadn't seen the owner of the black Lexus in a while and was wondering what he was doing at her godmother's house. Leah climbed out the car, letting the cool breeze kiss her skin. She smiled up at the house as her heart raced, trying to beat her to the front door. The boy inside was her heart's owner. Her heart needed him and was begging her to hurry inside. Leah let out a sharp breath and walked slowly up to the house. *What is he doing here?* As soon as her feet touched the porch, instant tears filled her eyes. She closed her eyes, letting them fall and then quickly swiping them away. Erasing any traces of emotions. Leah inhaled deeply and then exhaled slowly. She entered the house and the smell of chicken instantly filled her nostrils. She went into the kitchen and there he sat. Jamison. Her Jamison with his face buried in one of Stacy's old photo albums, looking at pictures of her from when she was a little girl. Leah smiled as she watched him be in complete awe of the sight of his birth mother.

Stacy was at the stove, doing what she did best and turned to see Leah standing in the doorway.

"Hey, baby girl."

Jamison looked up at the sound of Stacy's voice and a small grin formed at the corners of his mouth. He and Leah eyed each other for a moment like they were having a staring contest to see who would blink first. Jamison's eyebrow raised and Leah bit into her bottom lip and looked away.

"Hi, g mommy," she said, focusing her attention on Stacy.

Stacy smirked as she watched them. Her son and her goddaughter. The two people that she loved more than anything, because they were hers and now, they loved each other.

"Stacy, if it's okay with you, I'd like to step outside with her," Jamison said in a low tone, never taking his eyes off his sweetie.

Leah rolled eyes down to Jamison and then back to her godmother.

"Go head Bre'Ana. Y'all have a lot to talk about." Stacy urged.

Leah nodded and then looked to Jamison who was now standing in her space. The scent of him was beginning to drive her crazy as she stared up at him. Jamison reached out, seizing Leah's hand, lacing his fingers through hers.

"Talk to me."

"Okay," Leah whispered as he led her from the kitchen and out the front door.

Jamison began walking down the steps and then stopped. Leah took a seat on the porch as Jamison stood in front of her on the last step. He stared at her. Taking her in, from head to toe. Her beauty always fascinated him. She was exquisite and he missed the hell out of her. Going almost a month without seeing her was brutal. The inner battle he had with himself to not answer her call or to not reach out to her was hell. Jamison laid in bed at night imagining her laying right next to him. He wanted to go to her so many times, but the realization that Stacy was his mother stopped him from doing so.

"I'm sorry for the way I disappeared on you, sweetie."

Leah looked down at her feet and then rolled hurt eyes back up to him.

"It's okay," she said.

Jamison shook his head. He knew it wasn't okay. He knew it was wrong of him to neglect her the way that he did. He was hurting her each time he declined her call or let a message go without responding and he knew this because he would get a slight ache in his chest each time.

"Naw. It's not okay sweetie. I hurt you and I never in my fucking life wanted to hurt you."

He seized her hand and pulled her up from the step. Jamison pulled her into him and pecked her on the forehead. Leah closed her eyes. His lips were soft. She relished in this moment because she missed his touch. She missed the shield he provided. She just missed him period. Leah knew this with them was meant to be because of the way he made her feel each time in his presence. His love for her radiated from him and it could always be felt.

"Up." He commanded.

Without reluctance, she did as she was told and wrapped her legs around his waist. She stared at him as she waited for him to speak.

"I'm sorry baby. Real talk. I never should have played you to the left like that and I feel like shit behind it."

Leah tugged at his long braids causing him to give away a smirk.

"I can't really blame you. The devastation behind finding out something that deep couldn't have been easy. So, I understand. I can't lie, I was hurt but I understand that you needed time to process it all." She said.

"I missed the fuck out of your handsome ass though."

Jamison smiled as white teeth bit into his lower lip. *This girl*, he thought. He hadn't heard her say those words in so long and he missed it. Leah was the one to call him something other than a pretty boy and her compliment held more value than any other chick that had ever offered him one. She held more value than every chick that he had ever encountered. She was the one that had made him feel new, like a new version of himself. Leah had been the one to love him differently and captured his heart. She just touched him in ways that he never imagined.

Leah smiled.

"Why are you looking like that?" she quizzed.

Jamison silenced her with a kiss. A kiss that was long overdue because it had been too long since he felt that type of intimacy from her. Leah moaned as she slid her tongue into his mouth. The hunger and passion that was coming from this kiss made it feel like they were kissing for the first time. It was intense and there was nothing but desire behind it. A desire for one another that neither of them could ever deny.

Leah pulled back eyes still closed as she rested her forehead against his. She massaged the back of his neck as he caressed her back.

"So, what is it with us?" she whispered.

"Like can we do this, now that we know my g mommy is your mother."

The front door flew open and Leah immediately hopped down from Jamison's frame. They both stared up at Stacy. She smiled as she looked back and forth between them.

"Y'all get in here."

Leah and Jamison followed the order and went straight inside. They followed behind Stacy as she led them in. Stacy took a seat on the couch and she instructed them to have a seat on the love seat. They both sat and looked at each other. Jamison, with not a care in the world took Leah by the hand, intertwining his fingers with hers. Her instant comfort. Stacy watched, witnessing nothing but love.

"This situation is crazy. Trust me I know. I'm apologizing to both of you for the part I play in making it complicated."

"It's not complicated Stacy." Jamison spoke up.

"Nothing about it is complicated. I love Leah. You didn't raise me, you raised her. Just cause I now know you are the one that birthed me doesn't matter. I'm going to love her still and I still want her regardless. She's mine and even knowing who you are to me doesn't affect that. Now if we were raised as god brother and sister then I could see how it would be complicated. How it would not be right, but we weren't, so it is what it is."

Leah and Stacy both looked at him in stun because they both feared how he would feel. How he would feel about what others thought because they themselves had those fears. Jamison was uncaring of what the world thought. Their thoughts didn't matter. He was standing solid on what he wanted. He loved Leah too much to let go. She was his happiness. She provided something that no one has ever been able to give him. Love. Love so pure and that felt so good, it didn't seem like it could be real. It almost felt like a dream and if he were dreaming, he didn't want to come out of this dream. He'd rather stay in dreamland with her where her love would always be.

"Are you sure Jamison?" Stacy asked.

She wanted to be sure that he was truly okay with their situation. She loved them both, but she didn't want Leah hurting behind him being indecisive. Hell, she didn't want either of them being hurt behind a decision that wasn't thought all the way through. One thing Stacy was going to learn about her son is that he said what he meant and meant what he said. He didn't speak just because he liked the sound of his voice, he spoke the truth at all times.

"I'm more than sure," he said as he looked at Leah.

"You still mine?"

His words came out as if it were a question, but it was really a statement. Leah was his. His heart belonged to her and hers belonged to him. She wasn't going anywhere, and neither was he. To be without her was not going to be an option and Jamison was robbing Leah of her choice to respond.

"Yeah, you're mine," he said with a wink.

He leaned in and kissed her. He didn't care about Stacy

sitting in front of them. They were all grown and it ain't like she never saw a kiss before.

"Well damn," Stacy said laughing.

"Just forget the fact I'm sitting here."

Leah and Jamison both laughed. Leah buried her face in the middle of his chest as she smiled.

"Bre'Ana. You okay with this?" Stacy asked, getting back serious.

Leah nodded.

"I am. I know how it may look to others but like he said you didn't raise him. We didn't grow up in the same house and we're not blood. We have you in common, but those three things make it okay for us to continue this."

Stacy stood.

"Okay as long as we're all on the same page." She said as she headed for the kitchen.

"I'm about to make these sides real quick, then y'all can come in here and eat."

Stacy returned to the kitchen, leaving Leah and Jamison alone. Leah leaned her head on Jamison's shoulder as she gave his hand a gentle squeeze. She closed her eyes as her mind wandered. Leah didn't notice that a single tear had escaped until she felt Jamison wiping at her face.

"Don't cry, baby. We going to be fine. All of this will be okay."

Leah lifted her head and peered up at him.

"What if people start having something to say?"

Jamison smirked.

"Don't act like we're committing a sin or something sweetie. You just said it yourself. We weren't raised in the same house, I didn't know you until last year and to keep it all the way real, Stacy your mom. She just gave birth to me. I don't know her."

His last few words hurt to say but he was speaking nothing but realness. He wouldn't allow Leah or anyone else to make their outcome feel weird or wrong because there was nothing wrong with them loving each other. Their love was fair game and he planned to play it by any means necessary no matter what anyone said. He had vowed to love her. He vowed that it would always be him and her. No one else mattered because their love was that strong. It was destined for them to be together. Jamison knew it, shit he felt it. Why else would they have crossed paths? He had made it his goal to give Leah his last name and just because they had to jump a hurdle didn't mean a damn thing because he was still determined to reach his goal.

"I love you, Leah. We have nowhere to go from here but straight ahead. We not looking back sweetie. Let's leave all this shit in the rearview mirror."

"Okay." She said.

Jamison cocked his head back.

"Just okay?" he said with a raised eyebrow.

"And I love you too." She said rolling her eyes playfully.

Jamison shook his head and pulled her into his lap.

"Don't make me fuck you up." He whispered as he peeked into the kitchen and then back to her with seduction in his eyes.

Leah threw her head back as she laughed. She looked back down and the smile on Jamison's face warmed her. *Handsome self.* She pecked his lips as she stared at him. Leah didn't know how things were going to go from here, she just hoped that she didn't have to endure being without him again because this last time was torture. It had crippled her. She could barely sleep at night since he was away and just knowing that he was hurting behind the twist in their life, hurt her. She had missed the love he provided her. The constant shield he covered her with. Jamison was simply amazing. A true definition of a man who she was certain that she couldn't live without. It would pain her to even try. She was grateful that he was back in her life and she hoped that he was there to stay. Leah had enough of people leaving. Her mother had left her, her father had left her, and Marcus had left. Though she really left him. Leah just wanted Jamison to stay. She wanted him to be around forever. She had once heard nothing last forever, but she was determined to have this for eternity.

CHAPTER 8

*M*arcus walked in Chrissy's living room and shook his head at the sight before him. His son and his daughter. The families that he created with two different women. One he loved and the other he cared for, but he could never love because his heart was trapped with Leah. He walked up on Ma'Laysia who was in her brother's face and smiled.

"Lay what you doing baby?" he asked, scooping her up.

"Your brother trying to sleep, baby."

Chrissy walked out from the kitchen, joining them.

"She hasn't left his side since he went to sleep. She just been staring at him ever since I laid him down."

Marcus took a seat on the couch and held his daughter to his chest. This environment he was in didn't feel right. Even though it was the one he made, it still didn't feel right. Something was missing. Someone was missing. The girl standing in front of him didn't belong. Leah was supposed to be the one that gave birth to his son. He didn't want this. Marcus loved his son but his mama he couldn't love her. It was normally the women who loved the kid but regretted the daddy. However, in this situation, it was Marcus loving the baby and regretting the mother. Ma'Laysia climbed down and got back in the baby's face, she was in complete awe of him. Chrissy smiled and then looked to Marcus. She didn't miss the fact that he had completely ignored her.

"You and Lay staying another night?" she asked.

Marcus looked up and sighed. He didn't know what it was, he just couldn't bring himself to be that emotionally attached to Chrissy. Leah held his heart, despite the fact that she was now allowing the next nigga to hold hers. Instant pain filled Marcus as he closed his eyes and then looked down at his daughter. He never knew that loving someone and then losing them to another man could hurt so much. His heart was broken. Every day he walked around stepping on the pieces he could never seem to sweep all up. It was always that one piece lingering around, that was so small it was the hardest to get out.

"Marcus!" Chrissy shouted.

His eyes popped open and he just stared at her, not saying a word. Marcus was growing tired of being in her presence. He stood from the couch and walked past her, heading for her bedroom to retrieve his and his daughter's belongings. Chrissy scoffed as he walked past her. *I know this muthafucka didn't,* she thought. She swiftly sat his daughter on the couch and made sure their son was secure. Chrissy quickly headed for her bedroom, where she saw him getting his things together. She stood in the doorway with her arms folded as she watched him for a moment. She couldn't believe that after all this time, he still couldn't shake Leah from his life. It was clear that she was moving on with her life and that it was now time for him to do the same. However, Marcus was failing to face the reality that their hourglass had cracked and emptied a long time ago. Their time had been expired and he was still trying to find a way to repair the glass and put the sand back in it. He had to put it back in because he and Leah were supposed to be forever.

"When are you going to get the fuck over her? She has moved on. She left you, Marcus." Chrissy whispered.

Marcus paused and laid burning eyes on her. Her truth had stopped him right in his tracks.

"Why can't you love me? I've been here, way before her and I'm still here loving you. I gave you a son, I gave you my all, and you refuse to love me like you do her. What does she have Marcus? What did she do for you to love her?"

Tears began to fall as Chrissy spoke. She had been riding with him since the day they met. She was always around, loving him and doing whatever he wanted her to do. Then Leah came along and snatched Marcus' attention away from her. She was fine with it at first because she and Marcus had an understanding that he wasn't with being in a relationship. He wanted her as his female homie with benefits. Chrissy agreed. She was fine with their arrangement but as time went on, she started developing feelings for him. She began to love him and couldn't control how she was feeling. When she realized Marcus loved Leah, she tried to turn her feelings off but couldn't and allowed him to go back and forth between them just so she could still be a part of his world.

Marcus approached her, standing right in her face. He was so close that she could smell the alcohol on his breath. Chrissy took a step back as she looked at him.

"Tell me why?" she whispered.

Marcus shook his head.

"You just not her. She showed me something different. My heart just responds different when she around. Don't get me wrong, I fucks with you Chris, but Leah that's my fucking bey."

SLAP

Marcus didn't see the slap coming. His head snapped to the right and he held the left side of his face. He looked at her and then grew remorseful.

"I fucking love you, and you strung me along for over two

years. I know that's your baby mama but so am I and I'm the one standing here fighting for your love while she off loving the next nigga."

Marcus walked in Chrissy's space and pulled her into him. He cared for her, but he just couldn't find it in him to love her. Leah had all his love and he refused to give up on trying to get her back. She was the best thing that had happened to him, well besides his kids. However, now that Chrissy had given him a son, he was beginning to take her feelings into consideration and didn't want to see her hurt.

"I do love you, Chris." He lied. Marcus swallowed hard after the words left his mouth. He knew they weren't true, but he had to say something to soothe her. He didn't mean to hurt her by saying what he said about Leah. However, it was the truth but seeing his words affect her the way that it had he knew now that he would need to be easy on her, he couldn't give it to her raw like he used to.

"I'm sorry Chris."

Chrissy looked up at him, she cupped his face and tried to kiss him. She kissed his full chocolate lips and then he pulled back.

"Marcus just give us one real shot. Love me please?" she pleaded.

She waited for his response with bated breath. Chrissy closed her eyes and placed her head inside his chest. She listened to the sound of his heart. It was beating fast and hard.

"Please." She whispered.

Marcus looked down at her and let out a deep breath. He lifted his head to the ceiling and then back down to her. He shook his head. Marcus knew he was about to regret his words but as he took in everything she had said, he knew he owed her a fair shot. He just hoped that it would help him get over Leah. She had been around, riding for him and loving him through it all. She was now the mother of his son and since he couldn't get it right with Leah, he finally thought just maybe he could get it right with her. Marcus kissed the top of her head and then pulled her from his chest.

"I got you," he said.

Chrissy beamed as she wiped her face. She jumped up and he caught her effortlessly. She kissed his lips, again and then smiled. She finally got her man, not knowing that she had just got him by default. Not knowing that it was still Leah he was still wanting but using her in attempts to try to get over his first love. Seeing Chrissy's smile made Marcus both feel good and fucked up at the same time. He shook his head and then the cries from their son caused him to put her down and go attend to his son.

Leah stood in her full-length mirror, admiring her curves. The side effects of weight gain from the Depo birth control had her filling out nicely and her birthday dress hugged her frame perfectly. Her 20th birthday had finally arrived, and she was excited for the night to come. She had woken up to breakfast in bed that morning, prepared by Jamison and a bouquet of money shaped in the form of flowers. As promised, he had gifted her with a gift every day for the last thirty days, even when they weren't speaking. He made sure she received a gift, even her daughter got a gift. Today marked the day when she would be getting the last present. The grand finale.

Leah finessed her long ponytail that sat on top of her head as she continued to examine herself in the mirror. She couldn't get over the black Dolce and Gabbana corset dress that Jamison had gifted her with, along with the gold 6-inch heels made by the same designer. He was stepping her game all the way up and turning her into a complete woman, showing her the finer things in life. She walked over to her dresser and picked up the little gold wrapped box. She removed the lid and a 3ct tennis bracelet laid inside. Leah smiled as she removed it from the box and clamped the sparkling bracelet around her wrist.

The doorbell chimed and she took one last look in the mirror before going to answer. Leah took hurried steps to the door because now the person at the door was ringing it as if they had lost their mind and she knew exactly who it was. Leah didn't have to check the peephole, she snatched the door open in haste.

"Bitch why are you ringing the damn doorbell like that?"

NuNu smiled as her eyes scanned Leah from head to toe. Her smile caused Leah to smile and she took a step back so that NuNu could fully examine her. She did a little dance and NuNu instantly got geeked.

"Fuck it up boo," NuNu said sticking her tongue out and putting her hands on her knees as she popped her backside.

"Do that shit Nu." Leah shot back.

The girls were geeked up as they laughed and egged each other on. NuNu stopped dancing, entered the house and they both stepped into the living room. NuNu walked in looking just as beautiful as Leah. Her hair was in huge curls and she was the shit with her white one strap dress on that showed every curve on her body. Red heels and red lipstick accompanied the dress giving NuNu a grown and sexy look. The girls had truly entered both motherhood and womanhood with grace. Their growth had been beautiful as they transitioned from high school girls to women. If you would have told them a year ago that this would be their life, they would have looked at you crazy. Being a mother and dating slightly older boys was never their plan however it was their outcome and they loved it. They were in love with men, with brothers that treated them good and they couldn't be happier.

"I thought you were meeting me at the club?" Leah asked as she went to retrieve her buzzing phone.

NuNu stepped out of her heels and took a seat on the couch.

"Ty told me to meet him here." She said.

"Them fucking heels were killing my feet."

Leah looked at NuNu with confusion on her face and then back down to her phone.

My Love- You and Nu's limo will be outside in 15 minutes. Me and Ty will be waiting at the club. Enjoy the ride sweetie. I love you...

"Jamison just said he's sending us a limo," Leah announced.

The limo arrived and the girls made their way to the club. It was a nice night out as the girls rode through the city, music blasting as they stood up hanging out the sunroof. Toledo was alive that night as they made their way to the club. When they pulled up to the building it looked as if they were pulling up to a movie premiere. There were huge lights outside, along with a red carpet and rope that led to the door. The girls looked at each other and smiled. Jamison had truly outdone himself for Leah. He spared nothing when it came to her and tonight showed. He was definitely showing her something she wasn't used to.

The driver exited the car, making her way around the limo. The limo door opened, Leah and NuNu looked at each other smirking. This was life. They were with ballers, fucking bosses who were getting ready to boss their life up. It was no half stepping when it came to the men and they were proving that tonight for Leah's 20th birthday. The girls stepped out and lights began to circle them, as if they just knew the woman of the night was present. Jamison and Tyson emerged from the building, leaving the door to the club wide open. They approached the girls and Jamison swept Leah off her feet. He lifted her into the air and then back down to her feet gently.

"Happy Birthday sweetie," he stated.

As if it were rehearsed everyone in the line screamed, "HAPPY BIRTHDAY!"

Leah yelped and smiled as she buried her face into Jamison's chest.

Jamison lifted her face from his chest and kissed her.

"It's your night baby. Let's get geeked up!"

On cue, the bass from the music inside the club echoed through both the club and the nights air.

> ### *Go, go, go, go, go, go, go shawty*
> ### *It's your birthday*
> ### *We gon' party like it's yo birthday*

Leah and NuNu heard the music and instantly took off. One hand raised as they rocked to the music while strutting in the club one behind the other snapping their fingers. A big banner with *Happy Birthday Leah* on it hung from the ceiling. The lights from the club danced to the beat of the music as the two made their way to the dance floor.

> ### *You can find me in the club, bottle full of bub*
> ### *Look mami I got the X if you into taking drugs*
> ### *I'm into having sex, I ain't into making love*

Leah was smiling from ear to ear, dancing as she received love from everyone that she knew in the club. Her and NuNu were rocking, being cute as they focused on one another having the time of their lives. That was until Jamison came into Leah's line of sight. All black everything, was his attire. His grown man swag couldn't be missed. The smell of Giorgio Armani filled Leah's nostrils the closer he got to her. *This nigga is everything*, she thought as she stopped dancing and watched him. It was like Jamison was moving in slow motion because Leah was stuck as she waited patiently for him to approach her. That's when the music switched to a throwback slow song and Leah noticed Jamison smirking as he walked into her space.

***Every time I see your face it makes me want to sing
And every time I think about your love
It drives me crazy***

Jamison took Leah by the hand and she looked back to NuNu smiling, as he led her to the middle of the dance floor.

"Aight, we got the boss and his boss lady in the building make room." The DJ announced as he pointed in Jamison's direction.

"Break her down JJ," NuNu shouted.

Leah buried her face in her free hand as Jamison spun around, one eyebrow hiked and a sexy grin on his face.

"What are you doing baby?" she asked, turning red and temperature rising.

"This night wouldn't be official without a dance from the prettiest lady in the building."

"Okay baby, you don't know your girl will break you down," Leah said laughing.

"And you don't look like the type to slow dance."

Jamison smirked. Leah didn't have a clue as to who this pretty boy was. He was a whole fucking stripper underneath that hood persona. He loved to dance, slow dance that is. Only if Leah knew that he would have her ass coming back to back the way he would hit that shit while dancing behind closed doors.

Jamison pulled her into him and began to sway side to side. Leah wrapped both arms around his neck and began snapping her fingers as she mumbled the words to the song.

Girl you are the love of my life babe
And I'd give it to you baby
You belong to me and only me
I belong to you (I belong)

Leah began to get into the groove of the beat as she bit into her bottom lip. Those hips of hers started to wind as she began to move her midsection. Left to right. Right to left. Jamison moved his hands down to her waist as he allowed her to lead them on the floor. Leah was sticking her tongue out moving seductively as she stared at him, all while keeping her hips rocking to the beat, causing Jamison to smile.

Say my lady
You are so fine
I wake up in the morning to see a smile on your face
(baby)

Jamison was now singing the words. These words specifically because it's exactly how he felt. He did the shit so smooth that Leah had to stop dancing and take a step back. Jamison swiped his nose and pointed at her.

You are the queen of my heart baby
I belong to you and you belong to me (yeah)

He tapped his chest at that part smiling and pulled her back into him. Chest to chest, cheek to cheek as they began to dance again. Jamison pulled back slightly and stared at her, mouthing the next words.

Girl you are the love of my life baby
All those cloudy days they fade away when you come
my way baby

Then he kissed her. Jamison kissed her like they were the only ones in the building. No one else mattered. Tongue all in her mouth. Leah was his heart. Being able to love her was the best thing in his life. He knew that being without her would have been hard. It was already torture at night when he laid in his bed staring at the ceiling wishing he could reach over and wrap his arms around her. He wished to just be able to touch her. Jamison felt the words to this song, and he hoped that Leah was taking the hint.

Jamison pulled back and peered at her. He shook his head, admiring the beautiful image in his presence.

"Man, I fucking love your fine ass," he stated.

Leah's thong was ruined. His words had broken the dam between her thighs. She took his hand and discreetly slid down her leg and then up the front of her dress. She leaned into his ear.

"And *WE*, fucking love your handsome ass." She said.

Jamison's dick bricked. He slid his middle finger inside her wet and groaned. Before Leah knew it, he was pulling her quickly through the crowd of people. NuNu watched and smirked, shaking her head as she watched Leah and Jamison disappear in the sea of people.

Tyson noticed her watching and smirked.

"Mind your business Lor Mama." He said smiling, already knowing what she was thinking.

NuNu looked at him and burst into laughter. She then kissed him as they got into the groove of the next song.

Looking good plenty tight
Is there room, any more room for me
In those jeans

Jamison led Leah to his office as she squealed from the newest song from her celebrity crush.

"This my shit." She said as she snapped to the song.

Jamison opened the office door and pulled Leah in. He backed her into the door and kissed her. Leah pushed him back. Backing him into his desk. She slowly raised her dress and slipped off her thong once he was trapped between her body and the wooden desk. The music still could be heard clearly and Leah planned to fuck her man to the beat of the song. Jamison wasn't about to get in her jeans, he was about to get under a dress and slide into the best flesh that ever gripped his manhood.

Jamison leaned back and Leah climbed him massaging the monster along the way. It grew and Leah was anticipating the private party between Ms. Muffin as Jamison called her sex and his monster. She was hoping he was ready to eat because it was moist and warm just like he liked it. She leaned in and kissed him and then he secured her in his arms and raised up from the desk, switching positions and laid her on the desk. It was her birthday, right? So, he was about to blow the candles out and eat that cake.

Leah moaned as soon as she felt his tongue meet her flesh. "Agh."

Jamison licked her clitoris, her labia, and then stuck his entire tongue in her vagina. His tongue began to stir her icing, whipping that shit because he didn't like buttercream. He released his throbbing pole from his pants and slid in her. Leah's entire back arched off the desk and she wrapped her hands around his neck and leaned up, causing Jamison to pick her up from the desk. He bounced her up and down on his dick, allowing her to make a mess everywhere as she came, hard.

"Damn," Jamison said. His eyes closed involuntarily, and he bit into his bottom lip.

Leah's walls contracted so tightly around his pole that he came within seconds after her. Making it the best quickie they both ever had. Leah panted as she clung to him.

"I'm ready for the after party," she whispered.

"It's whatever you want sweetie." He said pecking her nose and then kissing her lips.

The pair straightened their clothes and exited his office. They were blowing the building because the real party was about to take place at his home. They approached Tyson and NuNu.

"We about to bounce," Leah announced.

NuNu looked from her then to Jamison and smiled. She shook her head.

"Y'all so damn nasty, what about the party?" she asked.

Leah hit NuNu with her own words.

"Girl shut up. I'm finishing the party at home Nu. Now excuse you, cause I got shit to do."

Jamison and Tyson both chuckled. NuNu put a hand to her chest as if she were offended and grinned.

"Oh, my bad bitch, go do you then."

Leah laughed and then attempted to kiss NuNu's cheek but NuNu moved.

"You probably been back there sucking something," NuNu said laughing as she blew Leah an air kiss.

Tyson turned to her and shook his head and Leah smiled. She wasn't sucking a damn thing, but the idea didn't sound too bad. She blew NuNu a kiss back and then looped her arm through Jamison's and headed out the club. The limo was still parked out front and Jamison helped Leah inside and then gave the driver specific instructions before climbing in behind her.

Jamison opened the champagne that was sitting in a bucket on ice, pouring him and Leah a glass. He made a toast to her as they rode through the city heading to Leah's final gift for the evening before they turned it in for the night.

CHAPTER 9

*C*hels stood in the driveway to Jamison's home as she debated on if she should go knock on the door or not. She noticed his car in the driveway and knew he was inside. She was pregnant with another man's baby and yet she still wanted her high school sweetheart. They belonged together. That's what they had vowed to one another all those years ago and though she did promiscuous things in their relationship, she still wanted him. She needed her JJ to be by her side and continue to love her. He had been there since she was 15 years old and was all she knew. Chels took timid steps up the long driveway. When her feet hit the first step to his porch she paused. She had been here just a few weeks ago and he had slammed the door in her face, leaving her outside without hearing a word she had to say. When he did come out, he said what he had to say and then left.

"You done, fucked up Chels. He not going to listen to you." She tried to coach herself.

Her heart and mind were at war with one another. Her mind was screaming for her to leave but her heart was speaking a language that she was more fluent with. She followed her heart and finally knocked softly on the door. She could hear faint sounds of music through the door, so she knew he had to be inside. She looked down at the red and black roses she had for him and sighed.

"He probably in there with that young bitch." She hissed under her breath.

Just the thought of Leah caused her to grow enraged. She had lost him to a girl, not a woman but a girl. Chels couldn't stomach the thought of him being with her. She shook her head and proceeded to go around back. She knew ways to get into his home and she was going to do just that. She was going to claim back what was hers. What had been hers for years and until this young chick crossed his path. What Chels failed to realize is that she had made it easy for Leah to steal his heart.

Chels climbed through the side window that she had secretly popped a lock on and slid inside. She walked around his home, taking in the scene before her. Jamison had red and white rose petals scattered throughout the entire downstairs, and up the staircase. She slid off her shoes and tiptoed up the steps. The floorboard at the top creaked and she winced.

"Shit." She whispered.

She hoped like hell Jamison didn't hear her as she continued to make her way down the hall. His bedroom door was closed and the music playing behind the door was loud and the same song she heard at the front door was on repeat. Chels released the trapped air in her lungs and inhaled fresh air as she braced herself for what she was about to see. She slowly turned the knob on the door and pushed it open. To her surprise his room was empty. She let out a sigh of relief, but her mind instantly began to wander.

"Where the fuck is he?"

Chels went back into the hall, making her way to the bathroom. No Jamison. *Where the hell is this boy and what the hell he got going on?* she thought. She made her way back to his bedroom, turned the music down, and then laid across his rose petal covered bed. She didn't know where he was or what he had planned but she wasn't leaving until she talked to her man. She laid in his bed and played with the petals.

"He loves me. He loves me not. He loves me. He loves me not." She said as she dropped petals on the floor one by one.

Jamison and Leah pulled up to a beautiful two-story home. Leah was so wrapped up in laughing at the silly joke Jamison had just told that she hadn't even noticed the limo come to a stop. When she finally did, she looked out the window in confusion and then looked back to Jamison.

"Baby, where are we?" she asked as she looked back out the window once more.

The scene in front of her was beautiful. Leah could see the lake from where the limo was parked in the driveway and immediately went to get out.

"You bet not touch that door sweetheart." Jamison called out.

Leah released the handle as if it were hot. She knew better and giggled when she laid eyes back on him. Never would she ever touch a door as long as he was around. That's just how he was raised and he carried that teaching with him still. The driver got out of the car and opened their door. Jamison stepped out first and then extended his hand out to assist Leah from the car. She stepped out and looked around, taking in the view. The way the moon reflected off the river was beautiful. Leah took slow steps up the driveway until the entire backyard came into view.

"Where are we?" she asked once more.

Leah looked, noticing the double doors to the garage open, and her white Mercedes along with a black Lexus with a huge red bow on top inside.

"Jamison!" Leah yelled as she turned to face him.

When she spun around, he was standing there smirking with both arms extended and keys in each hand. Leah's mouth flew open in stun. *No fucking way*, she thought.

"It's your house and your extra car sweetie. I kind of thought you could match my fly with the black Lex." Jamison said with a half grin.

Leah rushed him. Damn near knocking him down the way she jumped on him. She planted kisses all over him and began to grind her hips against his manhood. Jamison groaned as his pipe began to react instantly to the friction. As bad as he wanted to take her, right there in the driveway, he wanted to get to his place where they would end the night. Where he had an entire grand finale planned.

"Sweetie, let's go take a look inside." He said.

Leah pulled back from kissing him and shook her head.

"We can look inside tomorrow. Right now, I'm ready to show you how much I appreciate you."

"You got it." He conceded.

Jamison carried Leah back to the awaiting limo and instructed the driver to take them to his place. It was a short drive to his home and Leah noticed that he had purchased her a home close to his. He had just moved her out the hood and into a beautiful area where she could raise her daughter. She smiled at the thought. Leah leaned in and pecked his lips.

"Thank you."

She caressed the side of his smooth face as she stared at him.

"You don't have to thank me, sweetie," Jamison stated simply.

Leah shook her head.

"I do though baby. This is everything. You're everything Jamison. So, thank you. Thank you for being you and loving me the way you do."

Jamison kissed her forehead.

"I love you sweetie."

"I love you more handsome man," Leah shot back.

When they arrived at his home, the driver opened their door and the couple stepped out. They intertwined their fingers and made their way up the long driveway heading inside to end the night indulging in one another.

CHAPTER 10

*J*amison opened the door to his home and watched Leah's face light up. She looked around at the rose petals scattered throughout the entire downstairs. The lights were dim, and candles flickered giving the room a romantic feel. The smell of French vanilla wafted throughout his home. Leah closed her eyes and breathed in deep. *He is nothing less than amazing,* she thought as she opened her eyes.

"You did all this for me?" she asked as she stepped into the living room.

"Everything I do is for you Leah."

Leah turned and laid shocked eyes on him. Jamison hardly ever called Leah by her first name, so hearing it now she knew he was serious.

"Every decision that I make from here on out will be about you and Lay. I want y'all to be my family. I'm not temporary Leah. I'm never leaving. You were made for me and this between us," he said pointing between the two of them.

"Was meant to be. Being without you all those weeks was torture and I refuse to be without you again. Do you trust me?"

Leah nodded her head as a stray tear slid down her face. Jamison shook his head and wiped at her face.

"Don't cry baby," he said cupping her face.

"Use that smartass mouth of yours and answer me."

Leah smacked her lips and then smiled.

"I trust you, handsome man."

Handsome man. Jamison didn't know what it was about her calling him handsome man, but it did something to him every time. He swept her off her feet, causing Leah to yelp as he headed for his bedroom.

Chels jumped up when she heard Leah's voice and heavy footsteps. She thought she was prepared to face him and who she knew would be accompanying him but now she was a ball of nerves. She looked around frantically and looked towards the closet. She had just been reduced down to an in the closet bitch and made her way to it. Chels quickly closed the door slightly as she waited for them to enter. She looked down at the roses she left on the floor and shook her head. *Shit,* she thought.

Jamison placed Leah on the bed and kneeled down to remove her heels. He kissed each foot after the heels were on the floor. He pulled Leah from the bed and took a step back. Leah started to speak and he held up a hand, silencing her. Chels watched as sweat beads began to form on her forehead. *Why the fuck is he silencing her?* She thought. She immediately started thinking of what she could say if she was to be discovered in this moment. She let out a low sigh of relief once Jamison began to speak again.

"Let's play a game." He said with a smirk.

Leah looked at him with a raised eyebrow and smirk of her own.

"You down?" he asked.

Leah nodded.

"Okay. Well, Simon says, take off your clothes." Jamison stated.

Leah ran her tongue across her teeth seductively as she began to remove her dress.

"Slowly." Jamison coached.

Leah shook her head.

"But that's not what Simon said, baby." She shot back as she peeled out the dress at her own pace.

Jamison grinned as he watched her come out of every piece of fabric that was on her body. She was so fucking beautiful that his heart skipped a beat as he watched her. Leah was growing into a beautiful woman and Jamison felt like the luckiest man in the world to have her in his life. Leah was fully naked, standing before him in her birthday suit. Jamison licked his lips as he rubbed his hands together. *This fucking girl,* he thought. Jamison swaggered over to his dresser and lit the small tea candles that sat on it, one by one. He walked over to his radio, finding a fitting song for the mood. The sound of Rome filled the room as he made his way over to cut the lights off before making his way back over to Leah. The candles illuminated the room as they flickered. Chels heart dipped as she sat confined to the closet watching the scene in front of her.

Now I know
Just what you need babe
Come on over here
Let me hold you
There's a few things
You just might not know sugar
I'm so into you
And I love to see you smile.

Leah smiled as she listened to the words to the song. She closed her eyes as the slow jam began to set the mood in the room.

"That's exactly what I wanted to see, sweetie." Jamison called out.

"Simon says, come to me." He stated.

Leah's eyes popped open and did exactly what she was told, as she slowly walked to him. Nothing but seduction was in her walk and Jamison's dick bricked as he watched her approach him. Leah stood in front of him, totally comfortable in her skin as she started to sway to the beat of the music.

"Simon says, turn around."

Again, Leah did as Simon said and turned around. She swung the ponytail over her shoulder and looked back at him seductively. Jamison took a step back as he admired her beauty from behind. He bit into his bottom lip. Everything about Leah turned him on. If he were thinking, he would have made her stay in the heels she was wearing but it was too late for all that. Just the sight of her from the back was magnificent. Leah began to swing her hips to the music again and Jamison let out a low groan.

"Damn."

Leah smiled at his reaction. Jamison slid out of his clothing and stepped right behind her. Leah felt nothing but hard, warm throbbing dick on her backside and she gasped. *That fucking monster*, she thought.

> ***Now take one moment***
> ***Baby let's take our time***
> ***We got all night***
> ***We can drink the finest of wine***
> ***Just take my rhythm***
> ***Take it in stride babe***
> ***I love to feel your body all over mine***

"Simon says, touch your toes," Jamison said, giving off the last command.

Leah bent over slowly and touched her toes. She was like the prettiest flower, blooming before his eyes.

"Spread them legs apart," Jamison said with authority.

"That's not what Simon said." Leah teased. Her voice was soft and enticing.

Jamison gave Leah a smack to her right ass cheek.

"Agh." She cried out.

"That's what Jamison said, sweetie."

Leah moaned at the bass in his voice and slid her legs apart. Jamison entered her dripping walls without further words being spoken. Nothing but music and moans filled the air as Jamison worked her from behind. He was serving her long, slow strokes. Giving her the dick inch by inch as he held on to her waist to keep her from falling over.

Jamison threw his head back in absolute pleasure as he enjoyed the sounds of Leah's moans mixed with the sound of Rome. He leaned over and trailed his tongue up and down her back. He never stopped his stroke as he kept his tongue planted on her skin. Chels watched from the closet. Eyes misting as she watched Jamison do things to Leah that he had never done to her. Her stomach was in knots. She wanted to run out of the closet, but her feet were like cement bricks planted to the ground.

I've got to make you
Feel just what it is
I love I love I love
I gotta make you call my name

Leah was right on cue with it.

"JAMISON!" she called out.

"Agh." She moaned

Jamison looked down at the marvelous sight before him and smirked. He slapped her ass and then rubbed it soothingly three times like she was his genie. In this moment, she was and he was waiting on her to grant him a wish to allow her love to come down all over him. He wanted nothing more than to please her.

I've got to make you feel just right baby
I love to hear you moan
I love to hear you groan
My baby, oh
Just once, once more, three times baby

"Shit." He groaned as he lifted Leah making her stand upright and then leading her to the bed. Once her back hit the rose petals, Jamison hovered over her and slid right back in her. Leah gasped. She always gasped because she would never get used to his girth as it stretched her. She bit into her bottom lip as her eyes closed involuntarily and her back arched off the bed. Jamison was making nothing but love to her body as he worked to bring her to an orgasm.

I've got to make you feel just right baby
I love to hear you moan
I love to hear you groan
My baby, oh
Just once, once more, three times baby

Jamison's last stroke sent her over the edge.
"Give me that sweet shit baby." He coached
His baritone in her ear drove her wild as she climaxed all over his throbbing manhood. She began to work her middle as she enjoyed the ripples of ecstasy, causing Jamison to stiffen and then release an explosion within her walls.
"Damn." He grunted as he kissed the side of her neck and

then circled it with his tongue. He was intensifying her satisfaction and it caused her to shutter. Leah caressed his back as he laid on top of her trying to compose himself.

"That shit felt different," Jamison said in a low tone.

Leah smiled.

"It did baby." She agreed.

Jamison lifted and pulled Leah up with him. They climbed under the covers and allowed the exhaustion from the night to take them under. Jamison had made Leah's birthday one to remember and she would forever be grateful for him. Leah opened her eyes slightly and kissed his lips before drifting back off to sleep.

CHAPTER 11

*C*hels watched their entire night as a mixture of jealousy, hurt, and rage coursed through her. She was silent as she watched the love of her life do things to another woman that he had never done to her. Jamison was different with Leah. He took his time with her. He kissed her in places that he hadn't kissed Chels. Tears slid down her face and if it weren't for the music that Jamison had on a loop, she was sure that her whimpers would have been heard. When they finally fell asleep, she crept out of the closet and watched them. Jamison was comfortable with Leah, she could tell. The way he held her pissed Chels off because he was holding on as if he were scared, she would go somewhere. *He never held me like that*, she thought.

Chels shook her head as she walked to his side of the bed and tugged at his braids. Jamison groaned as he slowly began to open his eyes. When Chels came into view he hurriedly sat up and looked down at Leah who was sleeping peacefully.

"Man, Chels, What the fuck you on?" he asked as he looked back down at Leah once more and then quickly but quietly slid out of bed.

Chels took a step back, arms folded as she stared down at his manhood, which was semi erect and then up to him.

"Chels, I'm giving you until the count of ten to get the fuck out my shit before I do something I regret." He ordered as he slid into his boxers.

"No. Not until you talk to me." She demanded, louder than Jamison appreciated.

"Are you fucking crazy?" he said trying to hush her and push her out the room. If Leah woke up to this mess it would be some shit and he knew it. The last time the two women were under his roof hands were flying and he certainly didn't want that, especially with one being pregnant. Allowing women to fight had never been his thing and though Chels was asking for this ass whooping that would come, he couldn't let it play out the way.

"About you, you damn right I am," she stated.

Jamison got her into the hallway and closed his door. He pulled her towards the steps, and she stopped, allowing her weight to act as her strength.

"What the fuck is wrong with you? Huh!" he barked.

"JJ why can't you just give me another chance?" she pleaded as tears began to fall.

Jamison shook his head.

"Are you fucking crazy? You pregnant by another nigga. You had your chance. We're done. The girl I want is laying in my bed right now."

"We can get past that JJ. Just come back to me please," Chels pleaded.

"I can't watch you be with her or anyone else for that matter. Seeing you make love to her made me sick to my stomach."

Jamison's eyes grew wide. He backed up slightly and just stared at her for a brief moment. Then Jamison rushed Chels, backing her up into the wall.

"What the fuck is wrong with?" he asked.

"She wants her fucking ass beat, is what's wrong," Leah stated.

She emerged from his bedroom, wrapping her ponytail up. She had heard the entire conversation before they had exited the bedroom. When they left out Leah slid out of bed and found a pair of Jamison's hoop shorts and a white beater, throwing them on.

Jamison heard Leah's voice and his stomach hollowed. This with Chels was going to cause an issue, he was certain. *Fuck*, he thought. He released Chels and immediately tried to restrain Leah.

"Sweetie. Clam down. Let me handle it." He said.

"Naw, I'm about to beat the fucking brakes off this bitch!" Leah spat as she looked at Chels from around his side.

"Bitch you ain't going to do shit!" Chels shouted

"That's my nigga. He's been mine since high school and will always be mine!"

Leah chuckled.

"That's cute. Real cute. But let's get one thing understood. This nigga is mine. Dick, mine. Heart, mine, and you my dear is old fucking news."

Leah pushed Jamison and it caught him off guard causing him to stumble. She ran up on Chels, but before either of them could throw a punch, he swooped Leah up and carried her back to his bedroom.

"Sweetie, let me handle this. I got it. No fighting baby. I don't want my woman fighting. She not even worth it. She the type that will try to press charges on you." Jamison stated.

"What the fuck ever. She better roll out or she going to get rode on and that's on everything I love Jamison."

Leah walked away, making her way back to the bed. Jamison left the room once more and found Chels still in the same spot.

"You got to go. The shit you on has got to stop. Don't

make me end this night with a regret Chels and this my last warning. Watch your fucking mouth when it comes to her."

Chels scoffed and shook her head. She could not believe he was standing there acting as if she didn't matter. As if he had never loved her. He had known Leah for all but 30 minutes and was forgetting all the years they had with one another. She had taken Jamison for granted, thinking he would always be around. Chels toyed with his heart, playing with it and then putting it on a shelf when she was done as if it were nothing. She failed to take accountability for the agony she had caused him. While she was out sleeping with any and everyone, Jamison was out grinding and clueless to the shit she was doing until he caught her red handed. He came home, catching her with another nigga inside their home and fucking in their bed. Now the shoe was on the other foot and she had to witness him with someone else. The only difference was, they weren't together.

"Please, JJ."

"No," Jamison said cutting her off.

He marched her down the stairs, kicking and screaming. He led her to the front door and opened it for her.

"Get the fuck out. NOW." He barked.

"She better with her psychotic ass!" Leah yelled from the top step.

Jamison couldn't help the small chuckle that escaped his mouth. *She so fucking hard-headed man*, he thought. Jamison shook his head and looked up to see her standing by the steps.

"Simon says, shut your ass up and go back to the bedroom NOW, sweetie." He stated.

Leah turned on her heels and went back to the bedroom.

Jamison and Chels both watched as she disappeared. He looked back to Chels.

"Bye. We're done, don't fucking try me." He said with authority and a raised eyebrow.

Chels knew when that eyebrow lifted not to test Jamison.

She let a single tear escape and then quickly chased it away. She shook her head and exited his home without another word. However, the matter between him and her wouldn't be over until she got him back. *That bitch better watch, her fucking back*, she thought as she made her way down the driveway. She walked a block back to her car and with each step, she dropped a tear. Chels knew she was the cause of this, but she refused to give up and let go. Jamison was going to take her back one way or another.

"She what?" NuNu said sitting up in the bed, alarmed.

It was early in the morning as she listened as Leah told her everything that was going on. She slid out of bed and hurriedly went to her dresser to put on sweatpants and a t-shirt. *This bitch has lost her mind*, she thought. Chels had Leah fucked up and when she had Leah fucked up, she had NuNu fucked up. That's just how they got down.

"So, she still there?" NuNu whispered as she balanced the phone between her ear and her shoulder, sliding on socks before putting her shoes on. She looked to Tyson who was sleeping and then focused back on the task at hand. She grabbed the Vaseline off her dresser and attempted to creep toward the bedroom door. She knew that if Tyson woke up it would be over with. NuNu looked like a burglar the way she was tiptoeing towards the door.

"Nu'Asia!" Tyson barked.

"Busted." She said as she turned to face him.

"Yes, daddy." She whispered.

"Put the fucking Vaseline down and get back in the fucking bed. You not going anywhere and mind your business." He stated.

"But Ty." She began to plead.

"But Ty my ass."

He got up and crossed their bedroom. NuNu was forever in Leah's business and tonight Tyson wasn't having it. She would be staying her ass right in the house because he knew Jamison had it handled. He walked right into her space, his stare penetrated her and then he smirked. Tyson shook his head. *Her little ass*, he thought. He reached down, seizing her phone and placed it to his ear. He heard Leah calling NuNu's name and then he finally spoke.

"Put JJ on the phone boss." He ordered.

Tyson looked at NuNu and then nodded toward the bed. He didn't even have to say a word. She already knew what time it was. NuNu was silent. Mum was the fucking word as she made her way back to the bed, removing her clothes along the way. Tyson smirked as he watched her catch an attitude and then shook his head. *These girls be about that shit*, he thought.

Jamison finally got on the phone and Tyson immediately laughed as he listened to his brother talk about how the girls were crazy. Tyson knew firsthand they were nuts and that they didn't play about one another. That was one of the things that he admired about them. They always stuck together no matter who was right or who was wrong, they rolled together.

"Let me drop some act right off in Nu'Asia sneaky ass JJ and I'll holla at you in the morning."

Tyson said before hanging up the phone.

He looked to NuNu and smiled. He swaggered over to their bed and just stood there.

He stared at her and couldn't help the grin that spread across his face. She was his everything and he could never be upset with her for too long. Well except the time she accused him of some shit that she should have never even questioned. Other than that, NuNu was his pride and joy outside of their son.

"What?" she said with an attitude.

"Ard lor mama. You can chill with the attitude. You always in somebody mix."

"No. That bitch that tried to baby trap JJ all in Leah mix and I don't like it!" NuNu spat back.

"Nu'Asia shut up and let me mix this pipe in that shit!"

NuNu's entire body went warm and a pulse started in between her thighs instantly. Tyson's mouth always got her to give into him, it never failed. The nigga was crass and didn't care. He said what he wanted to say and how he wanted to say it. NuNu loved that about him and just like that she was dripping for him.

"Yes, daddy."

CHAPTER 12

ONE WEEK LATER

*J*amison and Leah rolled through the city with Leah behind the wheel of his drop top Cutlass. The top was down on the car as Leah's freshly pressed wrap blew in the wind. The day was beautiful, and Leah couldn't wait to leave her doctor's appointment, so they could get back to their day's plans. Jamison looked at Leah as she snapped her fingers to one of the city's up and coming R&B artist, The Rarebreed. Leah had attended school with the singer and he always walked through the halls singing to all the pretty girls, Leah and NuNu included. He just smiled as he watched her get lost in the lyrics. He was glad that she hadn't left him, like she done previous times after an encounter with Chels. Leah had stayed and Jamison appreciated her for it. Jamison hadn't heard from Chels since that night and was hoping that she had finally got the hint that they were done.

"We good baby?" Leah asked as she noticed him in his thoughts

Jamison smiled. He reached out for her hand and placed it to his lips.

"Yeah, we're good." He assured.

"We better be." She shot back.

Jamison shook his head. *This girl mouth so damn smart,* he thought. He loved everything about Leah, including her flip lip. Leah pulled up to Cordelia Martin, known for having the best female gynecologist on hand. Once Leah was parked, she looked at Jamison smiling.

"You sure you want to come in here?" She asked.

Jamison, nodded. He really didn't want her to get her tri monthly birth control shot, but it wasn't his choice to control how she felt. They had talked about her getting her birth control renewed the previous night and Jamison protested. However, Leah wasn't ready for anymore, kids at the moment. She was ready to start Cosmetology school because she had dreams of owning her own shop one day. She had explained to him that had life with Marcus not been so hard, she would have been started taking the course. When she admitted to her dreams, he could do nothing but respect her even more for standing firm on what she truly, wanted.

"Let's go, sweetie," he stated.

Leah went to open her door and paused before Jamison could even get his words out.

"I see you starting to finally catch on." He said with a smirk.

Jamison popped out of the car, making his way to Leah's door. He opened it for her and then assisted her out of the seat. Leah looped her arm through his as they made their way inside the building. Leah walked straight to the front counter and signed in. She was instructed to have a seat and that she would be called shortly. They waited in the waiting room for all of ten minutes before she was called.

They followed the nurse's assistant down the hall and Jamison grabbed a handful of Leah's behind.

"Boy," she yelped as she turned back to him and punched him in the chest.

"Damn," Jamison said as he winced playfully, holding his chest.

Leah laughed as they walked into the room she was assigned to.

"The doctor will be in with you shortly, but first I need a urine sample and to check your height and weight.

Leah knew the routine. She wasn't at all surprised. She gave a sample and then got her height and weight checked. Leah stepped on the scale and her eyes widened. She stepped back down as she looked at the nurse. She stepped back up on it. Leah just knew she didn't see what she thought she saw. When she looked back down, she shook her head. The weight she had put on over the last few months instantly irritated her.

"It's one of the side effects from Depo, Leah." The nurse stated.

"Well, I need to get off this shit." Leah stated as she stepped back off the scale. She headed back to her room once she was done. Jamison sat in the rolling chair flipping through a magazine. She took a seat on the exam table. The nurse clipped her chart to the back of the door and made her exit.

"This my last time getting this damn shot!" Leah exclaimed

Jamison looked up from the magazine and smiled. Leah shook her head and lifted an eyebrow. She already knew what he was speculating in his mind and she was getting ready to burst his bubble.

"Naw playboy." She said smiling.

"This shot is making me gain weight, baby. I don't want to be big." She whined.

Jamison shook his head and rolled salty eyes up to the ceiling. Leah hollered. She knew he was thinking the total opposite of what she was meaning. She was flattered that he wanted a baby with her, but Leah and a new baby wouldn't mix. She was focused and now determined to accomplish her goals. She already had her daughter and to have another would only set her back from being able to get her licenses to do hair. Leah just wanted to start growing into who she was destined to be.

A knock at the door interrupted Leah from speaking her next words. Her doctor walked in and Leah beamed.

"Dr. Asad!"

Dr. Asad smiled as he shut the door behind him and grabbed her chart from the back of the door.

"How's my girl?" he asked as he turned to her.

He walked over to the rolling stool and took a seat in front of Leah.

"I'm fine but what are you doing here?" Leah asked.

"That's a long story." He said as he shook his head.

"So, who do we have here?" Dr. Asad asked as he looked at Jamison.

"I'm Jamison."

"Nice to meet you, Jamison," Dr. Asad said before turning his attention back to Leah.

He scanned her chart and nodded his head as he looked over everything in front of him. Leah watched as he scanned the papers.

"Dr. Asad, after this dosage, I think I want to switch back to the pills. I'm gaining weight with the shot and I don't like it." Leah stated.

Dr. Asad looked up from the chart and smiled. He shook his head.

"Well, it seems to me that the weight gain isn't coming from the birth control."

Leah cocked her head back. She was confused. *What the hell he mean?* She thought. Her doctor noticed the look on her face and grinned.

"You are pregnant, Leah." He stated.

Leah's eyes widened and her hands shot to her mouth.

"What?!" She shouted as she looked at Jamison, who was staring at the doctor with shocked eyes. Leah looked back to her doctor, but this time tears were falling as she began to cry. She just couldn't be pregnant. She just couldn't be. How? Leah was emotional as she broke down in the room. She buried her face in her hands and shook her head.

Jamison stood and picked her up from the exam table. Leah threw her arms around his neck and wrapped her legs around his tall frame. She sobbed as the doctor's words replayed in her head, over and over again. *This can't be happening*, she thought.

"Shhh," Jamison whispered with a smile on his face.

He looked down at the doctor.

"How did this happen if she is on the shot. I thought girls couldn't get pregnant on that?"

Dr. Asad nodded.

"The shot is 94% effective, but one out of a hundred women could conceive while on it. Leah is that one out of a hundred." He consulted.

Leah climbed down from Jamison and looked at him. She couldn't believe she was that one out of hundred. *Him and that fucking monster*, she thought. Nigga dick was so scary even the depo couldn't protect her womb. Jamison pecked her nose and then Leah punched him in the chest. He smiled at her and Leah shook her head. They just stared at one another. Emotions swirling in them that they never felt before. They had created life and Leah placed a hand to her midsection. She could no longer contain her tears as she allowed the water works to begin again. Jamison wiped at her face and shook his head.

"Don't." He demanded.

Leah had no words. Her mind was racing a thousand miles per minute as she thought of every possible thing that could go wrong. She began to fear judgement and what others would think about her being pregnant before her daughter's first birthday. Leah couldn't believe that she was pregnant again so soon. Now, she had children with two different men.

Leah wanted to be married before she even considered having another baby. She would be able to say she had a baby with her husband and not her boyfriend. She shook her head and then turned to the doctor.

"How far along am I?" she asked in a low tone.

Dr. Asad looked at her with sympathy.

"Well being that you conceived while on the birth control, we would need to do lab work to determine that."

Leah nodded and spun on her heels to face Jamison.

"I'm sorry sweetie. I know this isn't what you wanted right now." He offered.

Jamison could tell that the news of her being pregnant wasn't sitting too well with her. Though he was thrilled about the news, he knew Leah was not. Jamison closed his eyes and shook his head. The words that were about to leave his mouth would taste like shit, but he had to think of her and her future before his own wants. She was worth more than just cranking out babies. He was going to respect what she wanted, even if it meant he would be sacrificing a piece of what he craved. Family.

Leah could feel his next words and instant regret filled her. She didn't mean to take away from his excitement and it caused more tears to build up.

"Jamison look at me." She stated.

Jamison's eyes popped open and Leah could tell that he was fighting back his emotions.

"I'm not going to get rid of this baby, if that's what you're thinking," Leah whispered.

"Are you sure sweetie, I don't want to…"

"I'm sure handsome man." She said cutting him off.

A smile spread across Jamison's face and he lifted her from the ground. Leah squealed. Her words were an instant relief. Jamison buried his head in the crook of her neck and kissed her there. *Thank you.* Leah didn't hear his words, but she felt him mouth them.

"You're welcome baby," she said as she pulled his braids, causing him to pull back from her.

Leah got her blood work done and they waited for over an hour for the results. Leah and Jamison talked about what would be next for them. They came up with a solution about school for her and Jamison was down for supporting everything that she wanted to accomplish. His reassurance soothed Leah's racing mind. She was now somewhat excited about giving Jamison the family that he had always wanted. Once her results were back, it was concluded that she was four months pregnant. *That night in the damn driveway*, she thought. Leah couldn't believe that she hadn't noticed any changes in her. She had a slight pudge, but she had blamed that on all the holidays that passed and being too lazy to work out. With Ma'Laysia she stayed sick and fatigued all the time. However, this pregnancy was the complete opposite.

Jamison and Leah left the doctor's office after scheduling their next visit, because Jamison had let it be known that it was their baby and not just hers and he wanted to be included in everything pertaining to their baby. They went back and forth the entire drive to NuNu and Tyson's house about what the sex of the baby would be. Leah wanted another girl, but Jamison wanted a boy. A little Jamison. Leah rolled her eyes at the way he was doting over the thought of having a boy and then smiled. They pulled up to Tyson's and NuNu's place to tell them the news.

"I love you handsome," Leah stated before she reached for the door.

"You better not," Jamison said shaking his head.

He climbed out and swaggered over to her side of the car, opening her door. He kneeled in front of her and Leah rubbed down his hair as she smiled at him.

"I love you too Sweetie and thank you again."

"Stop thanking me, baby."

Jamison shook his head.

"Naw, I have to cause you willing to put your life on hold for the next five to seven months in order to give me something I've been waiting for my whole life. A real family."

Leah leaned in and kissed him. She kissed him deep and long before pulling back. She loved this boy and couldn't believe that in less than six months they were already at this point. Though she had a twinge of regret when they first heard the news, it was now gone. Jamison was deserving of this, of her and she was glad to be doing this with him. She was proud she was the one doing it for him.

Jamison stood and reached for her hand, helping her out of the car. They were now getting ready to head inside and tell their two favorite people their good news. Leah could hear NuNu's mouth. *Bitch that's what I'm talking about.* Leah shook her head because she knew them would be NuNu's exact words. She loved the idea of Leah and Jamison together. So, Leah was certain that she would love the thought of having another god child, but this time by someone she got along with.

Before they could even reach the porch good, NuNu swung the door open and was all smiles.

"Bitch, yo pregnant ass." She said.

"Good job shooting the club up JJ!"

Leah and Jamison both looked at each other, minds blown. How the hell NuNu knew she was pregnant had their minds gone.

"Nu'Asia!" Tyson called out.

"Mind your damn business lor mama."

"It ain't my fault she butt-dialed me," NuNu said in defense.

"Your lor ass should have hung up. Just fucking nosey yo." Tyson shot back.

Jamison and Leah hollered in laughter as they entered the house. Congratulations were in order for the couple. Leah was all smiles as she took in the love and thought of how her life had changed, for the better. She had someone who was loving her right, someone who wouldn't abuse her physically or mentally. The thought of finally having a happy ending caused her eyes to mist and she quickly sniffed her emotions away. Then she thought of Stacy. She would be having a grandchild from her son and Leah wondered how she would take the news.

CHAPTER 13

4 WEEKS LATER...

*C*hels sat in the restaurant as she waited for her guest to arrive. She was reduced down to having a meal at AppleBees because the person she was waiting on was cheap as hell. Chels shook her head at the thought of the man. *I can't believe this nigga got me pregnant.* She sat in the booth as she impatiently waited. He was fifteen minutes late and Chels was irritated at the audacity of this nigga. Her mind instantly went to Jamison and she smiled. He wouldn't dare have kept her waiting nor would she be eating at such a place. Jamison was a man that liked the finer things. He would have had her eating downtown on the river. However, those days were long gone and just the thought caused Chels eyes to mist.

Chels looked out the window and then down to her watch. *Where the fuck is he?* she thought. Just as the thought entered her mind, she saw him entering the front door. He spotted her immediately and made his way to her. Chels eyed him as he approached. He was fine as hell. There was no denying that. However, she couldn't believe she had given this nigga her body, not once but twice and now they were here. Getting ready to discuss having a baby. She shook her head as he smiled at her.

"Have a seat Marcus," Chels ordered.

Marcus took his seat and he stared at her. She looked a little different from the last time he saw her. The night when he had her in Tyson's and NuNu's basement flashed in his mind and he shook his head. Chels could tell he was thinking of that night because of the way he was eyeing her. She was happy that Tyson hadn't discovered who she was. He was so wrapped up in the baby that he didn't pay attention to who all had entered his car or his home. Even when she made her exit, he hadn't paid attention being that he had whisked NuNu away upstairs to calm her down. When he did that, she and Marcus both left. They went back to his place and had sex. Despite the night being as chaotic as it was, she still wanted to partake in him sexually. They continued their sexual relationship two months up until she found out she was pregnant. Marcus was dipping in her and Chrissy both and now having kids back to back. *Project twins.*

Chels shook her head at the memory and then took a sip of water.

"You want to tell me why you called me here?" Marcus asked.

He was tired of the staring game they were playing and was ready to get down to business. He hadn't seen Chels since the morning after their last encounter and now here he was in her presence but wasn't sure why.

"First of all. How did you like the little pictures I sent you of Jamison and your daughter's mother?" She quizzed.

Marcus' eyebrows lifted in shock.

"What the fuck is going on?" He asked

Chels smirked. She had followed Jamison to Marcus' house the night he stormed out of his home. She watched as he and Leah made love in his driveway. Her smirk slowly disappeared at the memory.

"What the fuck is going on?" he barked.

"Jamison is my high school's sweetheart and now your

fucking baby mother is with him. I want him back, but I also thought it was only right for me to tell you that I was pregnant."

"You what?" Marcus asked. He was taken aback by the news.

"If you were with the other nigga how you know that baby mine?"

Chels shook her head. She wished like hell that it wasn't Marcus's baby, but she and Jamison hadn't slept together unprotected in months before discovering she was pregnant. Marcus and Mont were the last two men that she slept with outside of him and knew for sure that she and Marcus had been careless. Their carelessness resulted in them sitting in the restaurant to talk about what would come next. Chels didn't want anything from him. Shit, she didn't even want the baby. She had every intention on getting an abortion after Jamison realized that she had tried to trap him. However, her mother wouldn't allow it. This would be her parent's first grandchild and they just couldn't let Chels get rid of their first grandbaby.

"Look, trust me you're the last nigga I want to pin a baby on. It's yours and I just thought you should know." Chels said.

"This baby isn't my concern right now. I want JJ back and you're going to help me."

Marcus leaned back in the booth and trained skeptical eyes on Chels. He wasn't sure where she was going with this conversation, but she had his attention. He wanted Leah so fair exchange wasn't robbery. He had Chrissy but she was a rebound. Someone that would keep him distracted from Leah. However, that wasn't working. She was becoming clingy and mushy. That type of affection just didn't feel right coming from her. Hell, nothing felt right coming from anyone if it weren't coming from Leah. Not even the baby Chels was carrying that she was trying to place on the back burner as if it were nothing. Marcus was only going to dismiss the conversation for now, but it would be further discussed. He sat back mind blown at how all this came about. He had nibbled down on Chels the same night Leah and Chrissy had fought in the night club. Now they were here, and both of their first loves had crossed paths and now were in love. *Toledo small as hell,* he thought.

"What you trying to do Chels?" Marcus asked as he reached in his pocket to silence his phone.

"I want you to take Jamison up top and make it seem like Leah turned you on to the lick." She leaned in and whispered.

"They will never suspect us two. I'll tell you shit that only she and I would know but he'd never think I'm the one who set it up."

Chels knew of Marcus many hustles and being a stick-up kid was one of them. He had slipped up and told her the night they met at a club and she had always kept it locked in her mental rolodex. She did that just in case Jamison spot ever got hit, she would know exactly who did it, if that time ever came. Now she was going to use his line of business for her own personal gain. She was stopping at nothing to get Jamison back and if this plan didn't work, she had others that she was willing to put into action.

"So, what you think?" she asked as she leaned back.

Marcus pondered on the offer. He wanted Leah back and Jamison was getting money. He was a club owner so Marcus knew for a fact that Jamison would be a sweet lick. However, Marcus wasn't a fool. He would have to think long and hard about what she was wanting him to do. She was willing to set up the man she was claiming to love. Anything could go wrong, and it would possibly fall back on Marcus. He didn't know Chels well enough to just jump head-first into some shit that could possibly go left.

"Yeah, let me get with my nigga's and I'll let you know. But back to this baby. What we going to do about that?" he asked.

Chels sighed.

"Honestly, I don't want to do nothing about it. You can sign your rights over for all I care."

"Man, don't fucking play with me," Marcus stated in a stern tone.

"Who's playing? I'm dead serious. If this shit works, do you think Jamison will really let me and you be happy parents to this baby."

"And what if it doesn't? Look" Marcus said swiping his nose.

"I don't play about my kids and ain't nobody worried about that nigga. So, again I ask what we going to do about this kid?"

Chels shook her head. She was impressed but also irritated by his words. She couldn't help but smirk though. A waiter came and asked could she take their order. Marcus looked at her and then to Chels.

"You might as well let me feed you." He stated.

They ordered food and finally got on common ground when it came to the baby that she was carrying. She couldn't believe that she was actually beginning to enjoy his company. Despite that they were getting along her mind still drifted to Jamison. She missed him terribly and couldn't believe that she had messed up her good thing. Men called women their good thing but, in her case, Jamison had been her good thing and she was his bad. She had disrespected him numerous times. The ultimate betrayal is when she was caught with the next nigga in their home. Jamison was furious that day. He shot the nigga in the foot. It taught him to never walk in another nigga house again. Things between them hadn't been the same since. No matter how much she pleaded Jamison just couldn't get past it.

Lena sat in the booth behind Chels and Marcus. She couldn't believe what she had just overheard. She was there with Leah's father and had heard Jamison's and Leah's name. Just like the ear hustling ass lady she was, she was eavesdropping in on the conversation all while Leah's father handled a phone call he had just received. She would be taking all the information to Stacy as soon as she got the chance. She and Stacy had been friends for years there was no way she would not let her know what was going on. However, right now she was at the restaurant to discuss her situation with Leah, with the man who helped create her. Lena had called him because she was wanting to repair things with Leah. She was wanting to know her granddaughter. Come to find out, her father hadn't known Leah even had a child. With this realization it really cut him deep to know that his daughter hadn't told him about his granddaughter. The thought of Leah being a mom and not allowing him or Lena to be involved put an ache in his chest.

"Eugene, what are we going to do about this issue with Leah?" Lena asked.

Eugene paused for a moment, giving Lena a look. She never was the one to back down and shot Eugene back the same stare. He then cut his conversation short. Once he hung up the phone, he focused his attention on her. Eugene was tall, light skinned, with almond shaped hazel eyes. A well-known man around the city. One of the oldest hustlers the game knew and now he was running the best Wash & Shine in the city. That's where everyone, who was anyone washed their cars and parlayed on the nice days. Lena had been the only woman to ever give him a child. Their only child, that they both abandoned.

"We fucked up with her Ena." He stated calling her by the name only he called her. He shook his head. He thought about the last time he saw Leah. It was over a year ago and he had done his usual. He popped up with money for her to go shopping with and then he was gone with the wind. Never stayed. Never stuck around once he felt like his part was done. Leah was their only child and yet they acted as if she was the burden. Like it pained them to have her. Now here they were growing older and had been cut out of their daughter's life. She had created life of her own and now was building a family that didn't include them.

Lena nodded her head. He was right and now it was time for them to go to her and fix it. It was time for them to put their selfish ways aside and be parents. Eugene stood from the booth and slid right next to Lena. He swiped at the lone tear that ran down her cheek. He knew her, they were once the best of friends. High school sweethearts that had moved too fast in life and allowed that fast life to let them abandon the only life that truly should have mattered. Their daughter.

"We fought," Lena said with a chuckle.

Eugene grimaced.

"Jog that by me again." He stated.

He couldn't believe what he had just heard. He didn't even find humor in the statement. Eugene was hoping that he had heard her wrong because there was no way he could have just heard that his two women had been fighting. Lena nodded and shrugged.

"How the fuck did it come to all that?" He asked.

"Me, being me and showing no compassion for the shit I did to my baby." Lena whispered.

"I know what we have to do but listen." She said as she peeked over her shoulder.

"The boy behind us, and you bet not look Gene." Lena ordered already knowing that he probably would look anyway.

"That's Leah's baby daddy and I just overheard them plotting to set the boy she's seeing now up, which is Stacy's son. We have to stop that."

Eugene heard the pair getting ready to leave and stood to address Marcus. He watched as the girl went ahead of him and then stared at the boy that had given his daughter a baby.

A baby that he hadn't known about and was ready to meet. He looked the boy up and down. Marcus noticed the stare and spoke up.

"What's up wit it?" Marcus asked as a mug crept on his face.

Eugene took a few steps forward in Marcus' direction. He didn't like how Marcus was acting like there was an issue before he even actually knew it was one. Eugene squared his shoulders and then swiped at his nose.

"You Leah's baby daddy?" Eugene asked as he heard Lena approaching from behind him.

Marcus looked the six-foot man up and down.

"Yeah. Why? You fucking her?" he asked automatically assuming the worse.

When Lena came into view his eyes widened. Leah looked just like the woman. He had never seen her mother before and knew right away that she had to be Leah's mom or a very close relative.

"That's my daughter young nigga." Eugene said baritone deep and laced with distaste.

Eugene could already tell what type of dude Marcus was and he cursed himself on the inside for not being around to show his daughter better. He was sure if he had, she would have never let a nigga like Marcus get the time of day. He shook his head again and then leaned down to whisper in Lena's ear. Lena smacked her lips and then rolled her eyes.

"I'm Leah's real mama by the way." She stated before turning to go back to her seat.

"Have a seat," Eugene demanded nodding back to the booth.

Marcus was reluctant but he did as he was asked. He let out a sharp breath as he took a seat and then watched as Eugene slid in on the other side. The two men were silent as they eyed one another. Eugene shook his head. He couldn't believe Leah had allowed this type of nigga to give her a baby.

I should have taught her the game, he thought. Eugene shook the thought from his mind and then proceeded with the conversation.

"So, I overheard you and the young lady plotting to set my daughter new man up."

Marcus looked at him shocked.

"Yeah, nigga. That shit is a dead fucking end. If I even hear about you going through with that plot, your mama going to have to buy your ass one cause, I'll have my hitters on your head."

Eugene scoffed. He wasn't this man anymore, but it was nigga's like Marcus that would make him dance on the line between the streets and being a man with a head on his shoulders.

"Why you and Leah not together anyway, y'all got a baby together but not a family."

Marcus swallowed hard. He didn't know why the presence of Leah's dad made him nervous, but it did. He looked at the man and then realized he was no one to fear. Marcus realized he didn't owe this man not one explanation. He was never there for Leah, so who was he to question him about anything. Marcus smirked and then shook his head.

"Naw, the question is why weren't you there for your daughter?"

Eugene flipped the entire table over and yoked Marcus up from the booth.

"Nigga. I will murder your ass in this fucking place." He said sneering.

Eugene was choking the life out of Marcus and it took for Lena to come up and say something to get him to snap out of his rage.

"Gene, no!" She shouted as she grabbed at his arms.

Eugene released Marcus and then punched him in the mouth. Marcus had struck a nerve with the statement he made and for that Eugene was making one of his own. Letting

Marcus know that he wasn't to be messed with. Eugene stood and shrugged his shoulders, fixing his clothing as he eyed Marcus.

"Let's go Gene, now!" Lena roared.

Eugene walked away as the people watched the commotion. He passed by the manager that was on the phone and hit the button on the receiver. The man looked at him in alarm.

"No need for them boys my man. I'm out," he stated.

With that, Eugene made his exit. He left Marcus with a busted lip and a clear note that their conversation wasn't over. Eugene would make sure to see him again. However, it was time for he and Lena to go correct things with their daughter because something was telling him that the nigga he just left in that restaurant with a bloody lip didn't do right by his baby girl and if his assumptions were right he would be leaving Leah without a father for her daughter.

CHAPTER 14

*L*eah felt the sun's rays coming through the blinds in her old room at Stacy's. She and Ma'Laysia had spent the night with Stacy. Leah pulled the cover over her face. She was pissed that it was morning already because she wasn't ready to get up just yet. Then the smell of sausage filled her nostrils, pulling her from the bed immediately. Leah sat up and yawned as she stretched her arms above her head. She made her way out of her room and went in the bathroom to wash her face and brush her teeth. When she was done, she stepped in the hall and heard Jamison's voice coming from the kitchen and then a laugh from Stacy. *What the hell is he doing here?* She thought.

When she reached the kitchen, Stacy was at the stove making a plate and Jamison had her daughter, allowing her to dance on the table. Ma'Laysia was clapping and moving her little body to beat that Jamison was producing from his mouth.

"Go, Lay, Go, Lay," Jamison said, cheering the baby on. Ma'Laysia clapped her hands smiling and began to stomp her little feet. Leah smirked and shook her head.

"Um good morning," Leah said announcing her presence.

"Good morning sweetie," Jamison said.

He didn't even look back at her as he continued to make beats with his mouth.

"Morning Bre'Ana," Stacy said as she turned to her.

"Have a seat." She said nodding to the table.

Leah took a seat at the table and watched as Jamison played with her daughter. She smiled. Leah wanted to be mad because she wasn't ready for this yet, but it actually felt good to see him interacting with her daughter. Their interaction felt natural, not forced. Leah had once wanted to wait until she knew he wasn't temporary. She was pregnant and he would now have to be around regardless, so the notion of even being mad went out the window. He wasn't temporary because they had created life and her daughter would be a part of the family they had created. The thought of her being pregnant reminded her that they hadn't told Stacy yet. Leah leaned over.

"When are we going to tell her about the..."

"I already know your ass pregnant Bre'Ana," Stacy said, stopping Leah mid-sentence.

Leah and Jamison both looked at her in stun.

"Both of y'all pick y'all lips up." She stated smiling as she walked over to them both with plates in each hand. Stacy sat the plates on the table. Pancakes, eggs, sausage and grits. Leah's mouth watered as she dug right in. Stacy took Ma'Laysia from Jamison and placed her in the highchair that sat next to the table. She sat a plate of pancakes, cut up into tiny pieces on the highchair and allowed her grandbaby to go to work.

"You told her?" Leah whispered.

"Leah stop that damn whispering," Stacy said before Jamison could even answer her. She definitely had them mama ears already knowing what was being said.

Stacy took a seat at the table. Leah and Jamison both

waited with bated breath for her to speak. She took a bite of her eggs and then cut into her pancakes and took a bite of them as well. Stacy could feel their eyes on her and she smirked. She looked up at them and then shook her head. These were her babies. Her babies, that was getting ready to give her another grandbaby. The thought alone warmed Stacy.

"G mommy!" Leah shouted.

Stacy laughed.

"Girl, what?" She said

"How did you know?"

"Leah, you could tell all in your face and the slight weight gain." Stacy said.

"Also, the day Jamison was here, he got sick out of nowhere."

Jamison looked at her in surprise. Stacy smirked.

"Yeah, I pay attention to all that."

Leah shook her head as she watched them have a mother and son encounter. She was still mind blown that Stacy was his mother. Her heart ached at the thought of what she had endured for it to come about but oddly she was glad that Jamison had been given life. Had he not been given the chance to live Leah wouldn't know what it would be like to be loved by him. He was rare. A rare gift that had been placed in her life under the craziest circumstance. Either way she was grateful for him and loved him with everything in her.

"Now the question is, how far along are you?" Stacy asked.

They all sat around talking about Leah and the new baby to come. Stacy was excited that Jamison was coming around more and more since the first day they talked. He was everything she thought he would be. She knew it wasn't easy on him, given that she raised Leah and not him, but he was so in love with Leah that he didn't hold an ounce of resentment

A. MARIE

toward her like she thought he would. Now the two people that she loved more than anything in the world were brought together to tie her to them both for a lifetime.

After breakfast, Leah and Jamison were glued to the couch watching an old movie as Stacy played with Ma'Laysia on the floor. Stacy looked up at them and smiled. She couldn't help but to smile every time they came into her line of sight. Most would have thought they were crazy for still wanting to be with one another, but Stacy found it to be beautiful. She looked at Jamison and the way he smiled caused her to cringe slightly. He looked like the man who had planted him as a seed in her involuntarily. She stood abruptly and fled to her room.

"What the hell just happened?" Leah asked as she looked down at her baby.

Jamison looked down at her and shrugged.

"Let me go…"

Jamison shook his head.

"I got it, sweetie." He said cutting her off.

Leah lifted and Jamison stood. He wanted to be the one to check on her. This is how he would get to bond with her more. He made his way down the hall and curled a finger to Stacy's door. He knocked softly. Jamison could hear soft cries and he opened her door before being given permission to enter. Stacy looked up to him with wet eyes.

"I'm fine." Stacy lied

"I'll be out in a minute." She said sniffing.

Jamison shook his head. He wanted to be mad that she even had the audacity to lie to his face like that. Especially when it was evident that something was wrong, but he let it roll off his back and took a seat at the edge of her bed anyway. He was going to make sure she was good before he left out that room.

"G." He called out.

He wasn't comfortable with calling her mama or Stacy, so he opted for G instead. Stacy froze and looked at him. Her son. The son that would always remind her that she was a victim to something that no girl or woman should ever have to experience.

"What's wrong?" he asked.

"And before you answer. Think about the relationship we're trying to build first. Don't shatter it before our foundation finish drying."

His words let Stacy know that he wasn't with the games and she respected him for his approach. However, how could she truly tell him that she was having a hard time facing him at times because he reminded her of the man who had wronged her? She didn't want him to become uncomfortable, but she also didn't want to have lies between them either. Stacy was stuck between a rock and hard place as her mind pandered how to let her words come out without sounding harsh.

She let out a sharp breath and then fisted her short hair. She shook her head from another memory. Jamison's father was the very reason why she even cut her hair. She no longer wanted it after he told her that he loved her hair while he was violating her. Tears began to fall freely, and she felt Jamison swipe at her face. She grabbed his hand and then smiled.

"When you smiled, I saw my mother's boyfriend." Stacy whispered.

Jamison started to stand but Stacy pulled at his arm, forcing him to sit back down. His reaction is exactly what she feared, and she quickly explained.

"No, Jamison." She said, shaking her head.

"We're not going to do any more of that. I'm sorry. This is going to be hard on both of us, but I want us to try to get through this together without ill will between us. You're my son and despite how you were conceived I still love you because you are the only human who knows what my heart sounds like from the inside. I loved you so much that I kept my promise to you and never had another baby regardless of me wanting one. You are my one and only besides Leah and I love you regardless."

Jamison's heart swelled and he leaned over in turmoil. This was his fear. Her looking at him and seeing the man that raped her. Since the day she had told him what happened it always stayed in the back of his mind that she would one day look at him and see his father. Jamison didn't think it would be so soon, but the day had come and now he didn't know how to handle it.

"Jamison, look at me," Stacy said firmly.

The way she said it came out motherly and it both warmed him and made him feel awkward. Jamison was truly torn in half on how to feel. He looked up at her. Her stare matching his.

"We're going to be fine. Okay." She said soothingly.

Jamison nodded. He was speechless and Stacy shook her head.

"Use your words, Jamison."

Jamison smiled. Now he knew where he got that from. He too was a firm believer in people using their words when being asked a question and hearing Stacy say it made him feel warm. Stacy stood and pulled him up with her, pulling his tall frame into her as she embraced him tightly.

"I love you boy." She said, pulling back.

"You mean that G?" Jamison quizzed.

Stacy craned her neck back and looked at him as if he were crazy.

"Um. Just cause I didn't raise you don't mean I don't love you boy. Don't get this twisted now."

Jamison chuckled.

"My bad G."

He pulled her back in for another hug and started to make his exit. He paused at the door.

"I got something to ask you about later." He stated.

"Okay," Stacy replied simply.

When Jamison opened the door, he saw Ma'Laysia crawling down the hall. He smiled as he took wide steps and scooped her up.

"Where you going LayBay?"

Ma'Laysia smiled and then pulled on his hair as he carried her back out into the living room. Leah had dozed off and he smiled as he looked down at her. She was beautiful as she laid on her side with one hand tucked between her thighs and the other resting up under her head. Jamison shook his head. Falling in love with her was the best thing he could have ever done. He looked back to Ma'Laysia.

"Mommy went to sleep on you LayBay. Huh?" Jamison asked as he bounced her up and down.

Stacy walked in the living room and grinned at Jamison and her granddaughter's interaction. She had no doubt in her mind that when the time came that he would be an amazing father. The way he was with Ma'Laysia proved just that. She stepped up and reached for her grandbaby and as usual Ma'Laysia reached for her back.

"That's how you feel LayBay?" Jamison said, smiling and shaking his head.

Stacy smiled. Jamison just didn't know, that when it came to Stacy, he didn't have a winning chance, not even Leah stood a chance against Stacy when it came to her daughter.

"It's time for her nap. We're about to go lay down for a while. You staying here with Bre'Ana or you leaving?" she asked as she patted the baby's back gently.

Jamison looked down at Leah and then back up to Stacy.

"You don't mind me being with her?"

Stacy rolled her eyes. She didn't know why he was asking. They were past the point of asking, hell a baby had been made now, so there was no point of asking permission for anything.

"Boy gone," She said shaking her head.

Jamison chuckled.

Stacy left the room and Jamison approached the couch. He looked down at Leah and couldn't help but smile. This was his baby, his sweetie and he loved her. Loved her with every fiber in his bones. She was truly his everything. What he felt for Leah, he had never felt before. The emotions he had swirling inside him caused his chest to tighten. Jamison kicked his shoes off and placed them neatly on the side of the couch. He slowly lifted Leah and then laid on the couch and she instantly laid right on his stomach. Her favorite place to be and was right back out. Jamison smiled down at her and then rubbed her head gently. He picked the remote up from off the floor and began flipping through the channels on the T.V. before drifting off to sleep himself.

A knock at the door pulled Jamison out of his sleep. He groaned as he looked down at Leah who was still sleeping. Stacy emerged from the back with Ma'Laysia on her hip. She hurried to the front door and pulled it open without looking to see who it was. When she opened the door, there stood Eugene and Lena. Jamison craned his neck toward the door and noticed Lena immediately. He nudged Leah gently.

"Sweetie." He called out in a low tone.

Leah stirred out of her sleep, lifting her head slightly and looked up at him.

"Yes, baby?" she said.

A smile spread across his face. The sight of Leah was breathtaking. He shook his head and then removed her messy hair out of her face. He leaned down and kissed her forehead, forgetting that others were present. Leah smiled until she heard her father's voice.

"Leah," Eugene called out.

Leah looked up in shock as she watched him walk further into the house. She was even more surprised when she saw Lena walking in behind him. *What the fuck?* She thought. Leah hadn't seen her parents together since she was a kid, so seeing them together now had her confused. Leah lifted from Jamison's stomach and peered at her parents and then to Stacy. She hadn't seen her father in over a year. There was no excitement about seeing either one of them and Leah was ready to flee the room. All types of emotions started coursing through her as she watched both Eugene and Lena eye her daughter.

"G mommy, what's going on?" Leah asked standing.

Jamison stood with her.

"Don't let them upset you sweetie," He whispered.

Leah nodded. She eyed her parents. Eugene looked and noticed Leah's stare. He let go of his granddaughter's fingers and approached his daughter. Nothing but remorse was all over his face. He walked into Leah's space and looked from her to Jamison and then back to his daughter. Eugene had been doing a lot of thinking and he realized that he had been a terrible father to his daughter. He knew he wasn't shit. Him or Lena. They had abandoned her, left her with a woman that hadn't raised her own child while they were off doing whatever. He then understood why Leah had never told him about his granddaughter. A grandbaby that instantly stole his heart the moment he laid eyes on her. He shook his head.

"I'm sorry Leah. Sorry for everything that I didn't do for you and for not being around." Eugene said, letting out a sharp breath.

He didn't know that apologizing to his daughter would be so hard. It didn't help that Leah was standing there, arms folded, lips poked out and looking completely unbothered.

"All I can say is I promise to do right by you, from this day forward and I would love to get to know little mama back there." He said with a small grin as he looked back at his granddaughter who was smacking Stacy's face.

Leah was trying her hardest not to cry. She didn't know if it was the pregnancy or his last statement that caused her to produce the tears, but they were threatening to spill. She loved her father, but he hadn't been around hardly ever and Leah felt that the money he use to give wasn't enough to make up for the time that she wanted from him, for the lessons that she wished he taught her. That he should have taught her, because if he had she certainly wouldn't have allowed Marcus to manipulate her for as long as he did, if at all. She would have known better.

Lena approached. Head lowered and tears of her own forming.

"I'm sorry, baby girl," Lena whispered.

Leah shook her head. She could no longer keep the emotions from running down her face. *This has to be a dream,* she thought. There was no way she was seeing both her parents and hearing both of them apologize. This just couldn't be happening. Why were they here now? She was 20 years old with a family of her own now. So, why were they standing right here, right now wanting to come back into her life? It had been nine years of neglect. It had been eleven years of nightmares and hurt that Leah dealt with. Leah felt Jamison rub her back and then wipe at her face. He kissed her cheek.

"It's okay, baby."

Leah buried her face into him as she sobbed. This moment was too overwhelming. It was too much for her to deal with right now. Jamison held her close and glared at her parents. Stacy stepped up.

"Gene this my son Jamison, Jamison this is Gene, Leah's dad." She said introducing the two men.

Eugene extended an arm for a shake and Jamison allowed

his hand to linger for a moment before giving him a firm handshake. Jamison wasn't really feeling the way things were going and he didn't want this type of stress on Leah. He led her back to the couch and they both took a seat. Eugene and Lena both watched in awe as they witnessed their daughter being loved on.

Stacy watched as Jamison went from cool to protective and knew that she would need to keep the house settled before things got out of hand. She quickly went to put Ma'Laysia in her playpen that sat inside her room and turned cartoons on for her to stay entertained just in case her toys no longer did the trick. When she returned Lena was talking and Leah was still buried in Jamison.

"Leah, please talk to us." Lena pleaded.

Stacy looked at her with skeptical eyes. Lena was doing a lot of pleading for someone who was just talking mad shit the last two times she came in contact with her daughter. So, this sudden wanting to be civil and apologize alarmed Stacy. She knew Lena. Lena didn't apologize for shit and now here she was saying she was sorry and wanting her daughter's forgiveness. Eugene's apology may have been sincere. However, Stacy knew Lena's was not. She could feel that Lena had something up her sleeve.

"Baby girl, look at me," Eugene stated in a low tone.

Leah lifted from Jamison and peered over at her father.

"Yes." She whispered

"We're sorry baby girl. I know our words don't mean shit right now but one day they will because our actions will prove that. Can we start over?"

Leah gazed between her mother and her father. She never imagined this day to come. She had been through so much in her life that she didn't want to be subjected to any more hurt. Leah had experienced enough of it and she wanted to avoid pain by any means necessary. Choosing to stay away from the two people that created her but failed to protect her, was her avoiding pain. However, she could see the remorse on her father. She could feel it, but Lena on the other hand. She couldn't feel remorse coming from her. She couldn't see it in her face like she could her father. Even if Leah could she didn't know if she had it in her to forgive her mother. She had wronged her the most. The type of trauma Leah endured being with Lena would forever be a permanent wound. She didn't think it would ever heal therefore it was hindering their relationship from healing and being repaired. Her father, she could forgive but her mother never. It just wasn't going to happen. *Not in this lifetime,* Leah thought.

"I forgive you dad, but Lena."

Leah paused and shook her head. Just the thought of what had happened to her triggered anger in her.

"She allowed shit to happen to me that I could never forgive her for. So, like I told her before. She's dead to me." Leah said voice barely audible.

Eugene looked to Lena and then back to his daughter. His eyebrows were dipped in confusion. *What shit?* He thought.

"Ena, what is she talking about?" Eugene asked.

Complete silence fell over the room. No one said a word. They all looked to Lena as they waited to hear her explain to Leah's father just what she was talking about. *He doesn't even know,* Leah thought shaking her head. She couldn't believe that her mother had never told him what had happened to her. She couldn't have or he wouldn't be standing there asking what was going on. This only added fuel to Leah's fire. It did nothing but pile more hate and resentment on the plate that Leah would always serve Lena.

"Ena!" Eugene barked.

Lena jumped at the tone of his voice.

"What the fuck is my daughter talking about?" he asked with impatience.

The moment Lena let a tear slide down her face is when Eugene knew that she had allowed some shit to happen to his daughter. Some foul shit that he knew had fucked his daughter's life up and knowing that she did and didn't tell him infuriated him. He yoked her up by the neck.

"Bitch you bet not be telling me you let one of your boyfriends touch my fucking baby. I know that's not what the fuck she is saying you let happen." He said sneering.

"I...I..."

Lena couldn't get her words out. Her heart was racing as she grabbed at his hands around her neck. Eugene was mad. He was so mad that Lena could see the devil dancing in his eyes. Eugene's nostrils flared and he gritted his teeth as he held her out in front of him.

"What the fuck is she saying you did Ena!" Eugene yelled.

"Did you let some nigga, touch my fucking baby?"

Eugene shook Lena. Trying to get the truth out of her. She had never told him anything. She had never uttered one word to him about her boyfriend's son molesting Leah.

"I'm sorry Gene." Lena whispered trying her hardest to pry his hands from her neck.

Leah shot up.

"Dad, no, stop." She cried.

"Jamison do something." Leah said, turning to him.

Jamison quickly stood to intervene. He approached Eugene slowly, standing off to the side as he tried to talk to him. He knew firsthand that when a man was angry not to touch him because things could very well get ugly and Jamison didn't want that.

"Yo, man let her go. Look at your daughter, she's crying." Jamison said in a low tone, nodding in Leah's direction. He was hoping like hell Eugene would begin to put his daughter's feelings first. He said it was a new start, so he would be able to start by doing this one thing. Simply letting Lena go.

Eugene looked at Leah. Her eyes were pleading with him and he shook his head. He released Lena and pushed her. He looked at her and was disgusted. Now he understood why there was a disconnection between the two. He comprehended why Leah could not forgive her, because he would never be able to forgive her for this. Eugene laid eyes back on his daughter. He didn't want this for her. He never wanted this for her and nothing, but regret seared through him.

"I'm sorry baby girl. I never knew she had allowed you to be touched." His voice cracked. The thought of someone causing harm to his daughter had gutted him. It made him feel lower than low because he had not been around to protect her. He had allowed the streets to take him away from the one person that should have mattered to him. The one person that needed his love, loyalty and protection. He had failed her and now he could hardly stand to be in her presence. Eugene felt as if he didn't deserve another chance any longer.

Jamison helped Lena up.

"Leah I'm sorry." She said holding her neck.

Leah had no words. She said what she meant, and she meant that Lena was dead to her. There was no undoing the pain that she had caused her. She couldn't forgive Lena and wouldn't. She shook her head and allowed Lena's words to fall on deaf ears. Eugene sniffed and headed for the front door. Guilt was pressing on him heavy and he couldn't face Leah any longer.

"Daddy, wait!" Leah shouted.

Eugene's feet halted. He froze right at the front door. He heard her but he still couldn't face her.

"Please don't leave." Leah pleaded.

A tear slid down her face as she started to walk toward him.

"Leah, no." He said stopping her in her tracks.

Eugene sniffed back his emotions. His heart ached as he opened the door and left without another word. He would forever feel as if he failed her as a father. As her first love because that's truly what he was supposed to be, her first love because all girls loved their daddy's. They were their hero's the first man that would ever show her how to be loved properly. The first man that would either keep her heart whole or break it and that's exactly what Eugene had done. Broke her heart and now he was running away from the pain he caused instead of mending what he broke. He was once again taking the easy way out. Walking out of her life yet again.

Leah shook her head as she watched the door close. Her eyes prickled and she darted for her room. Jamison was stuck between going after his sweetie or going after the man that had yet again broken his heart because that's who Leah was, his heart. His heart to protect. His heart to love always because no one had stuck around to do so. It was as if he were designed specifically for her because he was the only one who would always be there, no matter what. Yes, he had left once and couldn't sleep at night when he was away, he was incomplete. That's how Jamison knew that Leah was made for him as well, because in her presence he was whole. He looked from the hallway to the front door. *Fuck.*

Jamison let out a deep breath and headed for the door.

"Jamison," Stacy called.

"I'll be right back G." He stated, walking out of the door.

Jamison had to try to fix this. He felt obligated to mend everything that was a part of her. He stepped out on the porch and scrunched his face as the sunlight smacked him. He saw Leah's father getting in his car and called for him as he sprinted down the stairs. Eugene looked up and paused, stepping back out of the car.

"How do you want a fresh start with her, but you're running now?" Jamison said as he approached.

Eugene didn't know what it was about the young man, but he just had a gut feeling that his daughter would always be protected with him. Jamison just gave off that aura. It screamed at Eugene that he was the one for his daughter. He witnessed the love Jamison had for her while they were in the house and it was much different from the feeling he got while in Marcus' presence. An explanation wasn't owed to Jamison, but Eugene spoke to him anyway.

"Truth is young I'm ashamed of how I handled her. That's my only fucking daughter. My only child and I didn't do shit to protect her. What kind of man don't protect his offspring?" Eugene said, shaking his head. He didn't even give Jamison a chance to respond.

"A fucking coward." He stated with a chuckle.

"I'm a fucking a coward. I let the love of chasing money and pussy come before me taking care of my baby and protecting her."

Jamison stood in the middle of the street with his mind blown at what he was hearing. If he didn't know anything else, he knew when he saw a man with regret dripping from him. Leah's father had that shit oozing from him. Jamison dug his hands in his pocket as an uncomfortable silence fell between the two men. He didn't know what to say. Eugene became lost in his thoughts at what happened to his daughter. He couldn't believe that Lena had never told him. If she had they wouldn't be in this circumstance. Leah's life would have been better, because it would have made her father look at things from a different monocle.

"Look man, I can see this has fucked you up, but don't fuck Leah up even more by disappearing on her again. She's had enough of that. Nigga's leaving and beating on her. She…"

Eugene looked at him.

"Beating?" he said voice getting caught in his throat.

Jamison shook his. *This nigga don't know shit about his daughter,* he thought. He let out an exasperated breath. He shouldn't be the one explaining all this, but it was already said so he might as well finish.

"Yeah, her baby daddy used to put his hands on her."

"Bitch ass nigga." Jamison said under his breath, more to himself.

Eugene was livid. Jamison could practically see the steam escaping his ears. However, Marcus was the last thing Eugene should be worried about.

"But don't worry about that nigga. I got that shit covered. Just fix things with my baby. It's clear she loves you and wants you around. Don't run from her, don't leave her now. You've already missed so much, don't miss out on the best parts to come."

Jamison didn't know everything but from what he did know he had to speak on. Eugene nodded. The wisdom of this young man before him had him baffled. It was like Jamison was a young nigga with an old soul and he knew a thing or two. He hoped that Leah would keep him around because he like Jamison and only knew of him for every bit of five minutes. Eugene nodded again.

"Yeah, you're right. I won't leave her. But while I have you in front of me it's something, I want to chop it up with you about." Eugene announced.

The men talked outside of Stacy's home for a half hour. The information that Eugene was passing down to Jamison had him wanting to call Tyson and go push down on niggas. Jamison was heated. He made a mental note to get with Tyson once he handled this with Leah's parents because the shit he had just heard wouldn't get swept under the rug. He wouldn't be pushing down on the breaks with this one, no yielding because Jamison was never the one to stop for anyone.

They entered the house to find Lena getting ready to head out and that Leah hadn't returned to the living room. She had meant good on what she said and was standing firm on it. She wouldn't flex or bend for anyone. Jamison bypassed everyone and headed straight for Leah's room. It was now time to check on his sweetie. He pushed open her door to find her sleeping. Just like that, she had cried herself back to sleep. Jamison could tell she had been crying because she whimpered slightly. He climbed in the bed behind her and kissed the back of her head. She was his life. His whole heart and for her to be hurt caused him to be hurt. He wanted to make everything in her life right. Make everything perfect because in his eyes, Leah was perfect, and she deserved nothing less than a perfect life. He kissed her head one more time before whispering.

"I'll never leave. You're mine and we were meant to be."

CHAPTER 15

5 WEEKS LATER...

"*L*eah boo," NuNu called out as she stepped into Leah's home. She looked around and noticed that everything was finally packed up in her old place and ready to be moved to the new home Jamison bought her on her birthday. NuNu couldn't help but smile. Her best friend was finally happy. Finally, with a man that was going to love her the way she deserved. There would be no crying over Jamison. No rolling down on other girls over him because he loved Leah too much to ever cause her that type of pain. NuNu made her way to the kitchen where she found Leah sitting on top of the counters eating ice cream. Neapolitan to be exact because she would eat the chocolate and vanilla together and leave the strawberry for NuNu. It was their thing. She grabbed a spoon and hopped right up on the counter with her.

"Nuuu," Leah said dramatically.

NuNu dug her spoon right in the bucket and grabbed her half of the ice cream.

"Why aren't you dressed?" NuNu asked as she kicked her feet like a little kid after she put the ice cream in her mouth.

Leah looked at her confused. She had no plans today. She

was waiting on Jamison to come get her because they were supposed to be going on a simple dinner date. It had become their weekly routine. He would take her out every weekend to the restaurant of her choice. He was giving and showing her things that she never imagined.

"Dressed for what?" Leah said looking down at her simple bootcut jeans and V-neck t-shirt.

NuNu shook her head.

"Heffa let's got find you something else to wear. You not about to go anywhere with my brother looking like that." She scoffed.

"Looking like what?" Leah said smacking her lips.

"Looking like don't nobody love your simple ass." NuNu shot back.

Leah rolled stubborn eyes and slid off the counter, placing all white painted toes to the wood floors. She let NuNu lead her to the bedroom to find something that hadn't been packed up yet. NuNu rummaged through the clothes until she pieced something together. Leah showered again, dressed and allowed NuNu to apply loose curls to her fresh wrap. When she was done Leah stood in the mirror looking stunning. She wasn't sure why NuNu wanted her dressed to impress but it was better than what she planned to wear.

"Now, you look somebody's fine ass baby mama," NuNu said smiling.

Leah rolled her eyes. NuNu thought she was slick. She knew Leah had been down lately about the weight gain and the slightly swollen nose. It was like ever since she found out she was pregnant, she started noticing all the signs of pregnancy. So, the little makeover was necessary and much appreciated.

"Thanks, heffa." She said smiling as she picked up her phone.

Leah dialed Jamison's number and it went to voicemail. She looked down at the phone puzzled. *What the hell?* she thought. She tried again and this time it rang once and he picked it up but then hung it up.

"I know the fuck he didn't." Leah said.

NuNu looked up from her phone.

"What boo?"

"Jamison ass has been ignoring my calls for the last two hours and when I just called this time, he picked up then hung up." Leah said as she dialed his number again.

"He got me fucked up."

Leah paced the floor as she listened to the phone ring. Voicemail. Leah looked at the phone and scoffed. Her mind instantly began to wander. *What the fuck is he doing?* She thought.

"He probably busy, boo," NuNu stated already knowing where Leah's mind was going.

"No, that nigga been answering me all day and now all of a sudden he's picking up and then hanging up."

Leah's insecurities began to resurface as she thought about what he could be possibly doing. Why wasn't he answering? Was Jamison turning into the nigga that got in good and then turned into someone completely different? Marcus had started doing this very thing and turned out to be the one to cheat and put his hands, on women. Leah sighed. *I knew this shit was too good to be true.*

"Nu, you try to call him." Leah said.

NuNu looked at Leah with sympathy. She pulled out her phone and dialed Jamison's number. Again, he didn't answer. Leah shook her head as she looked on in disbelief. He was beginning to act just like a cheating ass nigga. She always had doubts about him, but she had pushed them to the back of her mind because he had never given her a reason to question his love for her. Right now, those doubts were clouding her head as she thought of him being with someone else. She couldn't help it, because why the hell was, he not picking up the phone.

NuNu shook her head and then dialed Tyson's number. Maybe he could get a hold of Jamison. No Answer.

"Ty's not answering either." She said.

Leah sighed in frustration. They were fine earlier that morning and now all of a sudden, he was moving different. She was pregnant and her hormones were starting to be all over the place. Leah couldn't help the runaway tear that slid down her caramel face. She quickly swiped it away.

"Nu, take me to find this nigga." Leah stated as she grabbed her house keys and a jacket.

NuNu smirked. Leah was pissed and though she knew that Leah could handle her own, she wouldn't dare allow her to be in harm's way. She was pregnant and for that very reason, NuNu knew she had to be her protector. She was with the beef whenever, especially over Leah. NuNu would always be down to ride and even though she liked Jamison, that was her brother, Leah would always come first. She was her sister and blood couldn't have made them any closer.

"Let's bounce," NuNu said as she grabbed her keys from the kitchen table.

The girls headed out the door and hopped in the car. Leah didn't even know where to begin looking but she would ride around until she found him. He was now her child's father and for some reason, he was showing her a side of him that she never expected. *This nigga better answer, this fucking phone*, she thought. She grabbed her phone out of her purse and went to Jamison's contact. *My Love*. She paused for a beat as her eyes read those two words over and over again. He was her love and now he was beginning to act like her lost. Why wasn't he answering? Was he with Chels? Leah finally called his number. Again. Again, he didn't answer. She shook her head as she tried her hardest not to release the tears that were building by the second slip from her pretty brown eyes. Jamison had come into her life, showing her that real men existed, just for him to turn around and now make them extinct. He had shown her what real love felt like, what real protection felt like and now he was displaying something else. Something that Leah never imagined he would.

Leah let out a deep sigh as she laid her head against the window watching as the city lights began to illuminate the streets. It was their date night and here he was standing her up.

"Nu can you try Ty one more time?" Leah asked as she kept her forehead pressed against the window.

NuNu did as asked. Leah piped up when she heard NuNu talking. NuNu peered at her and then focused back on the road. When she hung up, Leah could tell that she didn't have anything to report that she would want to hear.

"Ty, hasn't seen him but I have to go pick your god son up from Ty real quick boo. I'm sorry," NuNu said with sympathy.

They drove ten minutes in silence. Leah noticed them approaching Ottawa Park and instantly wondered why Tyson would have his son out so late at a park. NuNu pulled in the parking lot and cut the engine. To Leah's surprise, the park was alive. Cars were everywhere. Every car except the one she was hoping would be there just by chance. *Where the fuck is he?* Leah thought.

"I need your help getting him boo. Ty got the stroller and the bags." NuNu said.

Leah nodded and climbed out the car behind NuNu. NuNu was now back on the phone with Tyson as he gave her directions on where to meet him. The park was huge and there were people everywhere.

"They're under the gazebo he said," NuNu said pointing in the direction they needed to head toward.

The girls headed in the direction, taking the trail that would lead them to where Tyson and Baby Tyson were. As they got further along down the trail, Leah began to notice candles lighting up the walkway. *What the hell they got going on over here?* She thought. NuNu started to pick up her pace and Leah couldn't keep up.

"Heffa wait for me, damn," Leah stated.

Her words fell on deaf ears because NuNu practically ran to where she saw Tyson and her son. Leah gave up, taking her time. She thought of Jamison again and pulled her phone out to call him once again. *He better pick up this got damn phone*, she thought. His voicemail picked up and Leah was irritated. She listened to the greeting and when it was time for her to speak, she went all the way in.

"I don't know what your tall ass is doing but don't even start playing these types of games with me." Leah hung up the phone and slid it back in her pocket as she began to hear music coming from the gazebo.

Let's stay in love
Let's stay together
Let's stay devoted
Let's stay forever

When Leah got closer, she could see candles formed in the shape of a huge heart and a trail of red roses leading to it. Her heart began to speed up and her eyes widen. Leah's hands shot to her mouth and her eyes misted when she saw Jamison walk up in the middle of the candles.

Let's stay in love
Let's stay together
Let's stay, let's stay in love.

Leah walked under the gazebo and right up to Jamison. She could no longer keep her tears from raining down her face as she stared up at him. Jamison shot her a wink and then smirked.

Girl, I must confess
That you are the best I've ever had in my whole life
And I believe that love,
Just wouldn't be complete
Without you here beside me to guide me through
whatever comes my way.

"Kill the music," Jamison announced after the first verse to the song that was playing.

On cue, the volume to the music was turned down and people started coming out from all angles. Stacy walked up with Ma'Laysia in tow. Then Tyson, NuNu and Baby Ty. Then Eugene and Leah couldn't believe her eyes. Her chest instantly began to rock as she looked around at everyone's smiling faces. She buried her face in her hands and shook her head. Jamison gently pulled her hands away from her face and shook his head.

"No crying, baby." He said as he swiped at her face.

"Let me talk to you okay."

Leah breathed in deep, pulling her bottom lip into her mouth and nodded. Her leg bounced nervously as she waited to hear what Jamison had to say.

"Leah Bre'Ana I love you." Jamison started.

He shook his head. He never thought he could feel so strongly about anyone, but here came Leah. She made his heart thump to a beat that was the hardest beat he ever felt, the hardest beat he ever heard. The shit was raw. She was life and now was giving him life, giving him, a family and he wanted her for the rest of his life. The first day he called her *Mrs.* he knew she was going to be his wife someday, because Jamison had never uttered those words before, not even to Chels.

"With that being said, I want to give you everything. A complete family, a happy home, and husband that's going to be down for you and only you in a world where you're the only woman existing to me." Jamison's words began to crack as he choked on his emotions.

This was it, as he stared at Leah in this moment, he knew that he was making the right decision. He had chosen the right girl to let love him and to give him the family that he deserved. That they deserved with one another. Leah looked at him with misty eyes. His words to her ears was the best sound she had ever heard.

"Eugene, do I have permission to marry your daughter?"

"You do," Eugene answered.

Leah's hands were at her mouth as she watched and listened to Jamison in stun.

"G, do I have your permission to marry your daughter?" Jamison asked.

"Yes," Stacy said, stepping up to them with Ma'Laysia on her hip. She placed her granddaughter on her feet and smiled. Jamison kneeled in front of Ma'Laysia and smiled.

"LayBay, can I marry your mommy?" he asked pulling out a small, wrapped box.

Stacy squatted down, getting eye level with her.

"Say yes," She coached.

Ma'Laysia looked up at Jamison and clapped her hands together.

"No, no, no." She babbled.

Everyone burst into laughter and Jamison dropped his head, placing one hand to the ground and grinned.

"Girl say yes." Stacy and NuNu both said in unison as they nodded their head, coaching her.

"LayBay," Jamison called out, finally lifting his head to look at her.

"We going to try this one more time. Can I marry your mommy?"

She finally nodded and Jamison pulled the tiniest ring Leah had ever seen out of the box and placed the half carat on her daughter's finger. What nigga asked permission from a child? Jamison. She didn't even know why it came to her as a surprise. He was a different breed and she loved him so much more in this moment. Stacy picked Ma'Laysia back up and went back to her original spot, wiping at her eyes because she had never seen anything like the show her son was presenting.

Jamison stood and looked at Tyson. Tyson took a step forward with his world and handed Jamison another box. They slapped hands and gave each other a nod.

"Ty, do I have permission to marry your sister?" Jamison asked.

"Fa sho you do dummy," Tyson stated.

"And what about you nephew. Can I be your sister's stepdad and your god mom's husband?" Jamison asked.

"Give uncle JJ a pound if I can."

Jamison held out his fist and immediately Baby Tyson tapped it with his. They had rehearsed this for days. Jamison and Tyson were both relieved that he remembered what to do with the gesture.

Jamison finally turned back to Leah who was a crying mess. She was sniffing and wiping tears as she watched him in action. The man she loved had truly outdone himself and she couldn't be happier with the person she now knew she was meant to be with.

Jamison lowered to one knee and looked up at her.

"Leah Bre'Ana Williams, will you please marry me?"

Leah's chest rocked as she shook her head hysterically.

"Use that smart mouth sweetie." Jamison corrected with a grin.

Leah smiled.

"Yes, handsome man."

Jamison opened the box, revealing a 4ct diamond ring inside. Leah's eyes were as big as golf balls at the sight of the ring. The way the ring glistened under the candlelight was breathtaking. Jamison took the ring out the box and slid it onto her finger and then kissed it. He stood and Leah jumped on him.

"You can ignore the message I left on your phone handsome man." Leah said smiling.

Jamison smirked and then shook his head. He could only imagine what she had said.

"Yeah, okay."

Leah leaned in and kissed him. She kissed him so deep that his dick brick and the seat of her panties were becoming damp. She rolled her hips and Jamison groaned. Neither of them caring that it was people around. Stacy covered her granddaughters face and smiled.

"That's how your ass got pregnant," NuNu said shaking her head.

"And JJ your ass sure didn't ask me, but I'm going to let that slide." She said with a grin.

Tyson shook his head as everyone laughed.

"Nu'Asia, bring ya ass." He stated.

Leah beamed as she eyed the ring on her finger. She turned to get her daughter, but Eugene was stepping up to her. She took a step back and Jamison placed a hand on her waist.

"It's okay sweetie, let him make it right. You need it." He whispered.

This boy was magnificent. The concern and care he showed for her was amazing. Everything was about her. He had kept his word when he said that everything he did, would always be about her. Jamison knew that having her parents truly did mean a lot to her. He didn't want any more discord between them. He was unsuccessful with Lena, but he was able to reason with Eugene and get him to see it his way. There was no denying that Jamison was the best thing that had happened to Leah and she was the greatest thing that ever happened to him. They just went hand and hand. She was like his lucky dice that he used to shoot craps with, in the trap house and would take nigga's up top for their money.

Leah was his good luck charm. He pecked her nose and she smiled.

"It's okay." Jamison said once more for reassurance.

Leah nodded and then stepped back up to her father.

Silence was between them as they peered at each other. Leah had a million thoughts running through her mind. She couldn't believe he was here, but she was glad he was. She ran into him and Eugene scooped her up off her feet. Hugging her tight as he stroked her hair.

"I'm so sorry baby girl." He whispered.

Leah nodded as she cried on his shoulder. This was what she had been waiting on. Leah had been waiting for years to get genuine love from the man that should have shown her what real love felt like.

"Thank you, daddy." She whispered.

Eugene smiled.

"Thank you, baby girl. Thank you for giving me a chance to make this right."

Leah through dainty arms around her father and clung to him tightly. She was like the little girl that had finally got to see her daddy after a long day.

"I'm so proud of you and the woman you've turned into." Her father whispered.

"Thank you, so much."

They pulled away from their embrace and Leah wiped at her eyes. She looked to Jamison who was smiling at her and she released a small chuckle. Leah let out sharp breath as she rolled misted eyes up toward the ceiling.

"Ugh." She said as she removed the last traces of tears.

"Stop all that crying boo." NuNu said.

"Let me see that damn ring. My boo getting married."

Leah laughed and held out her hand. NuNu grabbed her hand and smiled.

"That's what I'm talking about JJ." NuNu stated.

Leah grinned as she wiggled her fingers. This was it. She

was getting her fairytale ending. A life with Jamison as his wife as his one. Leah was finally getting that first come love then come marriage while the baby was already baking in her oven. She was both excited and nervous, but nothing was overpowering her excitement. Jamison stepped up and lifted her from her feet. She looked down at him. He looked up at her.

"I love you sweetie." He whispered.

"I love you more, handsome man."

CHAPTER 16

2 WEEKS LATER

"He's what?!" Chels yelled into the phone. She couldn't believe what she was hearing on the other end of the line. This couldn't be happening. It couldn't be true. How had things got that far with them and it had only been 6 months? She barely knew him, hell he barely knew her and now they're engaged. Jamison had asked Leah to marry him and Chels was livid. Chels shook her head against the phone. She was in utter disbelief. Jamison had never even scratched at the surface of marriage with her and her heart ached. They had been together for ten years and not a word had been mentioned about matrimony. *I can't believe this shit,* she thought as she threw her phone.

Chels paced the floor as grief took over her. She cried a gut-wrenching cry as she thought about the news she just received. Her chest was so tight that it hurt. Her Jamison. Her JJ had moved on and was building a life with someone else. Chels tried her best to control her breathing and just couldn't. The devastation she felt behind this news was too massive. *Married,* she thought.

"Noooo." She cried. The words came from the pit of her stomach as she sobbed. Her first love. Her only love had packed up his love and was leaving her behind. They had been together since high school. She had met him when they were fifteen years old and they had been together ever since. That was a decade ago and now Jamison had found someone else and only after months of knowing her, he was ready to make her his wife. Chels didn't realize that when a man found that *one*, he did whatever it took to keep her. Leah was his one. Chels was delirious. She pulled at the sides of her head as tears ran down her face.

Her baby kicked and she punched herself in the stomach.

"Agh." She cried as she doubled over in pain.

She hit herself repeatedly, crying out as she crumbled to floor. She was going insane. All logic had fleeted and now insanity was taking residence.

"This is your fucking fault." She wailed, holding her stomach. Chels needed someone, anyone to blame for what she was going through right now. Anyone but herself. She buried her face in her hands and bawled. Her stomach was quaking, and her chest rocked from pain. She had never felt hurt like this before. Chels didn't know what to do with all these emotions.

"Jamison, noooo!" She screamed. Her cries were loud, so loud that she woke up the nigga that had been laying in her bed.

"What's wrong?" he asked. Voice deep and barely audible.

Chels looked up at him.

"Get the fuck out!"

She stood abruptly and went to the closet. She snatched down on the string for the light, turning it on. She doubled over as pain shot through her stomach. Chels took a deep breath and then released it slowly. She stood upright once the pain had passed and rambled through all her shoe boxes until she came across the one that held her chrome Beretta pistol in it. The man got up and went to move toward her and she pointed it directly to his forehead.

"I said get the fuck out."

The man threw his hands up in surrender and then reached to grab his belongings.

"Bitch your crazy." He said as he slid on his clothes.

She was now enraged. Her mind was no longer her own. It was someone else's as she stormed past him and headed for the front door, snatching up her purse and keys along the way. She was going to get her man back. She was making him come back home to her. Chels couldn't live without him and she refused to let Leah have him. *This nigga got me fucked up if he think I'm going to just let him marry this young bitch,* she thought. Chels got in her red mustang and pulled out of the driveway recklessly. She couldn't live without him and she refused to. She was making Jamison come back to her voluntarily or involuntarily.

Jamison walked in his bedroom with a Ginger Ale and crackers in his hands. Leah had been nauseous all day and these two things were the only items that seemed to help. Leah lay curled up in the middle of his California size king bed watching the classic movie *Skool Daze*. Jamison handed her the crackers and then cracked the seal to the drink before handing her that as well. Leah consumed a little of both before handing them back to him and getting right back into her movie. Jamison looked at her and grinned as he sat the stuff on the nightstand before climbing in bed right behind her to watch the movie.

He wrapped strong arms around her belly and rubbed. Leah's belly was growing by the day it seemed after finding out that she was carrying. They were just a week away from finding out what the gender of the baby would be, and Jamison was excited. He knew they were having a boy and couldn't wait to have a little duplicate of himself stomping around this earth to carry on his name. His legacy because he would definitely raise him to be just like him but better. A much better version. Jamison felt a nudge and lifted in stun.

"Did you feel that?" he said with nothing but excitement in his tone.

Leah smiled and shook her head. She always forgot that this was his first child, so everything about her pregnancy excited him. This was her second rodeo, so it didn't come to much as a surprise when she felt the flutter. However, it did make her smile knowing that she was giving Jamison his first experience. He climbed over her and put his face directly on the spot where he had felt the movement.

"Come on, move for daddy." He whispered.

Leah looked down at him and rubbed her hand through his wild hair.

"Come on Babyboy," Jamison said rubbing her belly again.

The baby nudged his face, stretching his mother's belly and Jamison beamed.

"I think he or she knows your voice," Leah said with a grin, followed by a yawn.

Jamison lifted Leah's shirt and kissed her stomach. His lips against her skin sent a chill throughout her body, causing her to quiver. He kept kissing her, making his way up to her breast and then circling taut nipples. Leah sucked in a deep breath and let a moan escape her lips. Jamison helped Leah come out of her shirt and then leaned down, kissing her forehead. He then kissed her lips and Leah went the extra mile, sticking her tongue into his mouth and allowing their tongues to slow dance. Jamison dick hardened and Leah reached down, stroking the longest pole she had ever seen.

Leah then rubbed his back as they continued to kiss. Jamison ran a hand down her stomach and then into the hole of his boxers that she always wore for pajamas. He slid one finger down her slit and pulled back a wet mess. Leah was soaked. Jamison sucked his teeth as he closed his eyes and shook his head. He couldn't come out of his basketball shorts fast enough he was so ready. Jamison slid in Leah with the quickness and she gasped.

"Agh," Leah whimpered as he rocked in and out of her. His dick, she would never get used to. It would always be like the first time, every time she got on the ride. Jamison had that dope dick and Leah stayed high. Jamison turned her on her side, back against his stomach as he stroked in and out of her nice and slow. Taking his time. Always taking his time because what was the point of rushing something that felt so damn good. He closed his eyes and then groaned.

"Shhitt."

Leah's sex was like no other. He had experienced plenty of girls. However, indulging in Leah was the best experience. Her love making was different. It was like she made love to his soul. Sparks coursed through him as he bit into his bottom lip. He lifted one leg, straight up and kissed up and down her calf, never stopping the stroke. He looked down and shook his head as he disappeared in and out of her. Wax on, wax off. She was coating him with the nectar that her woman hood produced, and he couldn't get enough. Leah moaned. She clawed at the sheets as her man served her the best medicine to help soothe her stomach. Fuck the ginger ale. Fuck the crackers. This monster was doing the job, scaring the pain right away.

Chels crept in the room quietly. Jamison and Leah were so busy making music that they hadn't heard her coming in. She tiptoed slowly as she approached the bed. The sight of them sickened her once again. Once again Jamison was being different with Leah. He was giving her affection from behind that he had never given her. Chels nose flared and she closed her eyes.

"Simon says pull out of the fucking pussy, JJ," Chels said mocking him. Referring back to the night he had played a sexual game of Simon says with Leah. Seeing him being intimate with Leah again was crucial and sent her into a rage. She hit him with the butt of the gun before he could even see what was going on.

Jamison was stunned as he fell over holding the back of his head. *What the fuck?* Leah screamed as she grabbed her shirt and scrambled against the headboard.

"Bitch you move and I'll blow your fucking head off!" Chels yelled.

Jamison shook off the blow and arose from the bed slowly. He staggered as he stood, still holding his head, trying to gather himself in order to gain control of the situation. He looked at Leah and then to Chels.

"Chels put the fucking gun down." He demanded.

Jamison grimaced, pulling his hand away from his head, checking for blood. Chels looked at him and then pointed the gun in his direction. She was angry as she looked at him standing in front of her naked. Dick semi-hard and images of him inside Leah just minutes ago. Her nose flared and she bit into her lip. Jamison had her fucked up. All the way fucked up if he thought for a second, she was just going to let him walk away from her for good. She had ten years invested into him and Chels wasn't letting this young girl come in and snatch that.

"Chels." Jamison barked.

BOOM.

Leah screamed as Chels let off a shot in Jamison's direction barely missing him. A warning to let him know that she was going to control this show. Jamison ducked slightly and stared at her.

"Shut up!" she screamed as she wiped tears from her face.

"I'm doing the fucking talking and you JJ, you're going to do the fucking listening."

"Okay. Okay." He said in surrender, lifting his hands in front of him.

"Get rid of the bitch JJ or this time when I pull the trigger, I won't fucking miss." Chels whispered behind gritted teeth.

Jamison was stupefied. He had never seen her like this and couldn't believe that she was taking things this far. He swallowed hard as he approached her slowly. He had to try his hardest to disarm her and rectify the situation. He refused to let Leah and his unborn baby be in danger. Jamison stepped up to Chels slowly with his hands raised.

"I'm tired of playing games with you JJ. I let you have your fun. Now." She said pointing the gun at Leah.

"It's time to cut the bitch loose."

Jamison nodded.

"I'm going to make her leave Chelly Chel." He said calling her by the nickname he gave her when they were only fifteen.

"But first give me the gun, you don't have to do this. You've made your point. A good fucking point because I see you won't let go, so I'm hoping that it means you've learned your lesson. Right?" Jamison said nodding his head. He didn't know if this manipulation would work but he was hoping it did and he was hoping that Leah knew him well enough to know not to take these words to heart because she was the only one he wanted.

"Right?" He said once more as he finally invaded her space allowing the Beretta to push into his chest.

Jamison tilted her chin and caused her to stare up at him.

"Have you learned your lesson doll?" he asked in a more, stern tone.

Chels nodded, becoming vulnerable just by him infiltrating her bubble. His touch always weakened her, so when he held her chin, she had turned into putty, snapping out of the rage. She kept the gun pointed at his chest.

"I just want another chance JJ. I'm sorry."

"Okay, you got that but first give me the gun," Jamison said calmly.

Leah sat against the head of the bed watching in shock.
Her heart was racing, fear had taken over. She shook her head
not believing what she was seeing. Chels was delusional. Not
only that she was pregnant with another man's baby but
wanting Leah's man. Leah had never been the type to bite her
tongue and she didn't want to start now, but she knew she had
to in order for her and her baby to stay alive. *Where are you Ty?*
she thought. Leah had discretely sent a message to Tyson.

**Leah- Ty, please get to Jamison's. Chels is here
with a gun.**

She was requesting his help. Leah knew that Tyson would
be able to handle this because right now Jamison was defense-
less. Chels phone buzzed in her back pocket. She reached for
it and Jamison thought it would be the perfect opportunity to
take the gun but Chels shook her head.

"Don't even fucking try it." She said, taking a step back
from him.

Leah noticed the door cracking open from the corner of
her eye. Instant relief filled her when she saw Tyson come into
view. She looked at Jamison and noticed that he was already
aware of what was going on. He kept his hands up as he
peered at Chels.

"I'm going to ask you one last time Chels, give me the
gun."

"You think I'm stupid. You got this bitch in here taking my
place JJ. I'm the one who has been with you. I'm the one who
has been loving you since we were kids and you got the nerve
to have this bitch in here, playing house." Chels spat.

She turned toward Leah and then…

BOOM

Tyson fired one shot in Chels shoulder. The hot led ripped
through her flesh and she dropped to the floor. She screamed
in pain, as she gripped her shoulder. Chels rolled to her side to
see Tyson and she gritted her teeth as she stared at him. Tyson
looked from Leah to Jamison and then turned around.

"Damn boss you could have told me y'all was exposed." He said, shaking his head.

They both were still naked, but Leah had her shirt covering her chest. He had already witnessed too much and didn't want NuNu walking in.

"Nu'Asia, stop right there." Tyson called out hearing her footsteps coming down the hall.

"She fucking better." Leah agreed.

She and Jamison quickly dressed. When Jamison was fully clothed, he bent down and assisted Chels up. He looked her over and shook his head. How had things come to this? She was acting obsessed. She was acting as if he had removed himself from her life for no reason. Had she kept what was only supposed to be his between him and her, they wouldn't be in this situation, or would they? The love Jamison had for Leah was extraordinary. He never felt anything like what he felt for her not even for Chels and they had been together for years.

"We have to get her some help. She's pregnant." Jamison announced.

"Her ass needs more than help her crazy ass needs a straightjacket" NuNu interjected.

Tyson shook his head.

"Not now lor mama chill."

NuNu rolled her eyes and then embraced Leah. She was glad they had got there in time. She pulled back from their hug and stared at her. Nothing but empathy lived in NuNu's gaze. If it weren't one thing it was another. It seemed as if Leah just couldn't catch a break. Chels phone buzzed and Leah looked down at it and frowned.

Marcus- Dude stop ignoring my calls, how you feeling today? Do the baby need anything?

Leah was baffled. *I know this ain't Marcus Marcus*, she

thought. She heard everyone around her moving and talking but her mind was wrapped around the message she was staring at. Was it her Marcus? Was he really that type of nigga that was going around fucking any and everything moving? Leah's mouth fell open as memories of the night she caught him in the basement with a girl flashed in her mind. She never really paid attention to the girl's face. Leah was too busy throwing hands, pregnant and all. She went deep into her memory of that night trying her hardest to grasp onto a mental picture of what the girl looked like from the side, before the drama had started. *Think Leah, think.* Leah kept rewinding and fast forwarding the part before she kicked the girl like it was her favorite movie on a VHS.

Leah was so into her thoughts that she hadn't noticed anything or heard anything. Not until she witnessed NuNu walk up on Chels and kick her in the shoulder she had been shot in.

"Stupid bitch!" NuNu screamed.

"Nu'Asia." Tyson barked.

"Nu'Asia my ass. Y'all not taking this psycho no fucking where. Call the bitch an ambulance."

When Leah seen Chels roll to her side that's when it hit her. That side view. *It is her*, she thought. The realization gutted Leah. She dropped the phone in disbelief. *This city is too fucking small.* Leah shook her head as she looked down at Chels. She had an overwhelming urge to jump on her but the flutters that were moving throughout her right now hindered her from doing so. Leah let a deep sigh and shook off the sting from the devastation.

"Jamison, call her an ambulance, but you're not taking this *HOE* nowhere." Leah's voice held nothing but finality as she put a lot of emphasis on hoe. She peered down at Chels. *I could beat this bitch ass.*

NuNu looked at Leah and smiled. She loved it when her

best friend talked that shit and NuNu wouldn't be NuNu if she didn't add her two cents that was hardly ever required.

"Y'all heard her." She said.

"Call her ambulance or honestly since the bitch wants to play with guns like she really about that life, shoot her and throw her in the fucking swamp with the…"

"Nu'Asia!"

Tyson looked at her. His eyes spoke and she knew she was going too far.

"That's E-Fucking-Nough!" He chastised.

Jamison peeked up at Leah. He saw the pain in her eyes. He saw the fear all in her face. He shook his head and rolled cold eyes back down to Chels. He held his t-shirt to the wound so she wouldn't bleed out. He pulled out his phone and placed the call. This entire situation was getting out of hand. Jamison knew that he needed to get a hold of it before it was too late. People were ending up dead and he didn't want to keep adding bodies to his resume. He didn't want any more harm coming Leah's way. It was time to dead all threats so he could move on and be happy with the family that he was creating. Starting with the situation he and Leah's father had discussed. There was no way he was going to allow Leah's baby's father to come and try to rob him. He was getting ready to stop him dead in his tracks. He only hated what it would potentially do to Leah. He wished there were another way to handle it, but shit was going left, and Jamison had always said if it went that way, he would make that shit right.

CHAPTER 17

The sun was blazing down on the court as the boys went through their normal routine of basketball games at Hamilton park. Everyone was out, it was a nice day and the city always came alive on nice days. The girls as usual were in attendance, bopping around trying to be seen as they were spectators to the games being held. DeShay watched as Mont ran up and down the court, putting in work. They had been seeing one another for the past 5 months and things were beginning to get heavy between them. Mont never exposed the dealings of any of his business with DeShay so she was clueless to the role he played in Dominic's disappearance. The family had put up ten thousand dollars for anyone to tell them about his whereabouts. They didn't know that it was Mont who had gave up Dominic's location to the enemy. It was Mont that had got his lady's brother killed.

When the game was over Mont slapped hands with his team and headed toward the bench where DeShay was sitting with her crew. He took his time walking toward her as he admired her from afar. It was never in his plans to fall for her. He had strict rules. Never fuck with the homies sisters because he wouldn't want any of them fucking with his, if he had one.

However, Mont had crossed that line and fell for Dominic's little sister. He not only fell for her but had also caused her pain that she was unaware of and a twinge of guilt seared through him as he approached her. Mont stepped in her space and she stood. DeShay looked him directly in the eyes and beamed when he licked his lips.

"Nice game baby." She complimented.

DeShay looked at him with lustful eyes. She was in complete awe of him. Mont stared at her and then shook his head. He was foul and he knew it. He had been straddling the fence for months. Dominic was his best friend, but he knew Jamison was the man and he knew that Jamison wasn't to be played with. Mont was stuck between a rock and a hard place not knowing what to do and had let a girl scratch at the surface of his heart.

"You know I'm the man." He said coolly.

DeShay smacked her lips and threw her arms around his neck.

"You're my man," she shot back.

She caressed the back of his wavy head and then pecked his lips. DeShay was head over hills for Mont. She hadn't noticed the attraction until the night of Leah and NuNu's graduation party. She was all smiles as they talked and laughed while tucked off in the corner of the hall. Mont was tough but he was also fun to be around. She always enjoyed him when he was around and now, here she was trying to be his rider. The girl he knew that could help him make it in life and be down for him.

Someone clearing their throat right behind Mont caused them to break apart. When DeShay pulled back her eyes widened in shock. Mont regarded the look on her face and instantly turned around. His eyes widened in horror. It was as if he were staring at a ghost. He knew what Jamison was capable of but to see the boy in front of him he began to question that.

"Nic," DeShay screamed.

She lunged for him causing him to stumble back slightly. She hadn't seen him in months. The entire family had been worried about him for months. They knew he was the rebel. He was the one that was always into something especially after what happened to Mandy. Now, here he was in the flesh.

"Where have you been?" she cried.

"We were worried sick about you."

The boy put his sister down on her feet and peered at Mont.

"I see you still can't tell me and Dominic apart, baby sister."

DeShay stepped back and took a second look. Her eyes misted when they landed on the small apple shaped birthmark on the boy's neck.

"Nicky!" She screamed.

Again, she leaped into his arms and buried her face into him. Nicholas caught his sister effortlessly. He was Dominic's twin. The youngest twin and the only way anyone could tell the boys apart was if they really paid attention to the birthmark. DeShay hadn't seen her brother in almost two years. Him and Dominic were split apart at birth. Their mother kept Dominic and Nicholas stayed with him and Dominic's dad. DeShay hadn't even known she had a twin brother until a few years ago. Nicholas and his father moved back to Toledo after his father retired from the army. The first thing Nicholas did was get reacquainted with his mom and twin brother. Then Nicholas went away to college and now was back home for the summer. He had wanted to surprise his mother and sister. The only one knew he was returning was Dominic and now he was nowhere to be found.

"I missed you, Shay Shay." He whispered, placing her on her feet.

"What's goodie MonTae." Nicholas said laying fire laced eyes on him.

Mont stepped up and slapped hands with Nicholas.

"What's goodie my nigga."

The boys bumped shoulders and then broke apart.

"I know what's not good is that I just caught Shay Shay kissing my homie," Nicholas stated talking to Mont but burning holes in his little sister. She shrank automatically already knowing that he wouldn't approve of the relationship.

"Nigga, you know that's against the code."

Mont nodded. Nicholas was right. He was breaking boy code like a muthafucka but he couldn't help it. She was the good to his bad and he appreciated the balance that she brought to his world. DeShay was the sunshine on his dark days and trust Mont had a lot of dark days. Losing his grandparents at the age of sixteen and living in their home alone forced him to take care of himself quicker than he expected. His mother was an addict who had died from an overdose when he was ten years old and he never knew his father. So now he was moving through this thing called life alone with no siblings, just a couple aunties, uncles and a few cousins scattered throughout the city. Mont was now twenty years old and had come along away and he knew he had an even longer way to go. However, with DeShay at his side he was certain that it would be worth trekking through because with her he felt something special.

"I know but your sister is special my nigga, and I don't want to fall out about it but shit she worth the trouble."

DeShay couldn't believe her ears, she was amazed that Mont had the courage to state how he felt to her brother. Mont didn't even tell her the words that he was speaking to her older sibling and the truth being revealed stunned her. She knew Nicholas would never take it left field because he was the more level-headed twin. The good twin, in fact the perfect twin. It was Dominic who was the off-balanced one and the one who would have wanted to fight about his little sister when it came to his nigga's.

Nicholas swiped his nose and nodded.

"Okay. Listen to me good though." Nicholas said as he stepped toe to toe with Mont.

"You hurt her and imma fuck you up nigga."

"I got her," Mont assured.

DeShay sighed in relief. She should have known that Nicholas would be the one that was more lenient and would have more understanding then Dominic. She felt like a burden had been lifted off her shoulders. She didn't want it to be any issues when it came to the two boys she loved. DeShay didn't want to be stuck choosing because just like any young girl she would choose her man.

The boys slapped hands again and then Nicholas turned to his sister.

"Where's your brother?" He asked.

DeShay's chest tightened and Mont steeled. It was moments like this that would always remind him of the foul play he done by giving up information on where Dominic was hiding out at. He knew once he had done that, Dominic's life was getting ready to expire because Tyson and Jamison were determined to eliminate the threat. He rolled over on his best friend to save his own life and lived with the regret of doing so every day.

"We haven't seen him in months, Nicky," DeShay admitted.

Nicholas looked at her in confusion.

"What?"

DeShay nodded. Nicholas didn't understand what was going on and the fact that his twin was missing in action alarmed him, especially knowing that Dominic loved the streets. Something was off and Nicholas knew it. Call it the twin intuition.

"Where's mother?" he quizzed.

"She's at work." His sister answered back.

Nicholas nodded and then he thought of *her*. He smiled

and shook his head. He missed her terribly and wondered how she was doing. He wanted to lay eyes on his love. He left her based on lies and it felt that he owed it to her to tell his truths. Nicholas shook his head, snapping out of his thoughts and training his focus back on his missing brother. He would go seeking her when the time was right and hoped that she would give him a chance to explain his true self and whereabouts. However, right now it was time to find his brother.

Chels opened heavy eyelids the next morning. Opening them slowly to the sound of a beeping heart monitor. She winced when she went to sit up in the bed causing her head to sink right back into the pillow. That is when she remembered the night before. She recalled hearing a blast and then slipping in and out of consciousness. She reached up and touched her injured shoulder. Chels shook her head and attempted to sit up again.

"You need rest Chels."

The voice came from the corner of the room. She looked over and noticed Marcus lifting from the chair he had been confined to. Chels let out a sigh. She wanted Jamison. Why wasn't he there with her? *It's his fault why I'm here. Had he not left we wouldn't be in this mess*, she thought.

"What are you doing here?" she asked.

"Are you or are you not pregnant with my baby? Cause if you're not I'll bounce." Marcus shot back.

He wasn't with the attitude or the games. He would gladly leave if she admitted that he wasn't the kid's father. Hell, that would be one less kid he would have to worry about because Marcus never wanted a bunch of kids by different women anyway. He already didn't know how he would tell Chrissy about this being that they were in a forced relationship. Chels rolled her eyes and released a harsh breath. She put an arm over her face as she began to think about Jamison. He was moving on with his life and leaving Chels behind because he had fallen in love with someone younger, someone she felt couldn't be compared to her and that couldn't love him more than her. Chels couldn't just let go. It was like deep down inside she was relying on hope. She felt like their love would never die. However, on Jamison's end Leah had blown out the flame on their candle of love. Leah had lit a new flame and the flickering of her light was much more mesmerizing to watch.

"Yes, but that don't mean shit. We don't have to play…"

Marcus held up a hand.

"Let's get one thing straight. I'm not trying to play shit. My heart belongs to Leah and she's the only one I want a family with. I'm just trying to do right by you since you say this baby is mine."

Just the mention of Leah's name pissed Chels off. She was green and not because she was sick. She grabbed the sides of her head and yanked at her hair screaming, from both pain and frustration.

"Agh," She yelled.

"Don't fucking mention her name to me. What is it with y'all and this bitch?"

Marcus looked at her slightly disturbed.

"Get out. Just get the fuck ouuuttt!"

Marcus backpedaled toward the door. He stopped just as he got ready to push down on the knob to make his exit. *This bitch is crazy*, he thought. She was acting as if nothing in the world mattered except Jamison. Marcus watched her as she went through fits. She was screaming and calling his name. There was a knock at the door. A doctor and then a nurse following behind him entered the room.

"Chelsyn we need you to calm down." The doctor said as he approached her bed.

"We don't need you adding extra stress to you or your baby"

Chels sobbed as she buried her face in her hands. She could care less about the baby she was carrying. The baby didn't belong to the man she wanted it to be with, so she simply didn't care. The only reason she even was still carrying the child was because of her parents. Had it not been for them, she would have aborted the baby and felt like she would have had a better chance of getting her man back. Chels felt a sharp pain bolt through her and screamed in agony. She grabbed her stomach and rolled to her side.

"Agh!" She cried.

Marcus immediately began to rush to her side.

"What's wrong?" he quizzed as the assisting nurse interfered.

"We need you to go wait in the hall sir. Everything should be fine." The nurse coached as she led Marcus out of the door.

Marcus was escorted out of the room and turned to face the open window that was in the middle of the door. He watched as the nurse and doctor performed work on Chels. He stretched his long chocolate arms across the door and leaned his forehead onto his forearm. Marcus kicked the door softly, *how the fuck did I end up in this shit.* Life wasn't supposed to be taking all the twists and turns that it was taking right now. Marcus had no clue what to do or how to get a grip on it. He was stuck in love with his first child's mother, forced himself into a relationship with the second child's mom, and now a third child was on the way with a woman who was crazy in love with the man his first love was now in love with. He was in one big web of love and Leah was in the center of it.

CHAPTER 18

2 WEEKS LATER

*J*amison pushed his black Lexus through the city streets, music bumping and speakers knocking. It felt good outside. He felt good. He had the prettiest girl on his right and his pistol resting on his left. He had hated to carry it, but the way things had been recently, he felt that he couldn't be without it. He and Leah just left their doctor's appointment because he meant what he said it was their baby and he would always be included. He couldn't be happier on this day. Today would mark the day he received the second-best news of his life. He and Leah were having a boy. *A fucking boy*, he thought. He peered over at Leah and grabbed her chin, forcing her to face him. She rolled those pretty brown eyes to him and smirked. Jamison stuck his tongue out and Leah mocked him. She had lost their bet and now was acting like the biggest brat Jamison had ever seen.

"You mad sweetie?" Jamison asked with a grin.

Leah folded her arms across her chest and poked her lips out.

"Hell, yeah cause I wanted to go to the damn club for the show. How y'all going to book my favorite singer and then not let me come baby. You know I love The Rarebreed."

Jamison shook his head and smiled. Leah was definitely a brat. The show was a month away and he knew she loved the singer; she was going rather she won the bet or not. He just wanted to make her sweat. Jamison loved it when Leah acted like that. With one hand on the steering wheel he used the other to unfold her arms and grab her hand. He brought it to his mouth and kissed it. Leah melted at the way his soft lips sunk into her hand.

"You lucky I love your bratty ass or you would be staying home. I don't want you out in the club with my son but since Breed is your favorite you get a pass." Jamison said.

Leah beamed. She leaned over and kissed the side of his face.

"I love you, handsome man."

Jamison smirked and his heart swelled. It was shit like that, that had him soft for her. The sentiments that she spoke to him rolled off her tongue so effortlessly and genuinely. She was caring and feeding him things that no one his age had. Leah was almost like a dream that he didn't want to wake up from just in case his reality wasn't real. She was that amazing. The simplest thing such as calling him handsome made Jamison love her that much more. She was easy to love and to be loved by her, Jamison felt was the biggest blessing. He would do anything in his power to keep her by his side because without her, he felt a void. A void that he knew for certain no one else could fill.

Jamison pulled in front of Tyson and NuNu's house. As usual after each appointment they went to his brother's house to let them know how things were going. Today they would be sharing the news of him having a son. His firstborn was a boy and he was beyond delighted. Jamison climbed out of the car and made his way to Leah's door to assist her out. He opened her door and extended an arm for her to latch onto.

"You didn't butt dial Nu's nosey ass this time, did you?" Jamison said with a chuckle.

Leah laughed so hard that her stomach quaked. NuNu was very nosey and Leah knew it.

"No, baby I didn't."

"Good, cause her ass spoiled it last time." Jamison shot back.

The couple made their way up to the door and like always it flew open. NuNu stood in the door with her hand on her hip and one hand out as to say *well spill the beans*. Leah shook her head as well as Jamison.

"Y'all not coming in unless y'all tell me it's a boy." NuNu stated.

"Girl shut the hell up and move. I got to pee."

NuNu stood there with her eyebrow raised.

"Nu'Asia." Tyson barked.

NuNu didn't say a word. She rolled her eyes and moved to the side. Tyson walked up to her and scooped her up. NuNu yelped in surprise. He put her over his shoulder and walked her over to the couch and slammed her right on it. Jamison and Leah burst out in laughter.

"Ty!" She screamed.

"Ty my ass you always doing something. Yo ass pick too much lor mama."

Leah walked past them and flipped NuNu off.

"That's what your big head ass get." She said as she made her way to the bathroom.

Jamison assisted her up the stairs and NuNu watched them as they went up the stairs.

"Y'all bet not get a quicky in while in my damn bathroom."

"Lor mama mind yours damn," Tyson demanded.

He shook his head as he watched her pout on the couch. She always had something to say. Always. Baby Tyson came running from the kitchen where he was at trying to get his basketball from up under the kitchen table. Tyson picked him up and spun him around in the air. *My world*, Tyson thought.

Flashes of the day at his party hit him, causing his eyes to sting with tears. Tyson had to sniff back his emotions. Leah and Jamison descended the stairs and took a seat on the opposite side of the room. NuNu looked at her, irritation all over her face. She knew Leah was being funny by doing all the whispering she was doing in Jamison's ear.

"Bitch, damn what is you having?" NuNu finally stated.

Leah smirked and looked at Tyson and her godson.

"Baby Ty," Leah cooed.

She reached her arms out for him and Baby Tyson wiggled until his daddy released him. Jamison and Tyson both shook their heads. The girls were childish with one another. Tyson watched as his son ran over to Leah and jumped right in her lap. He cried when he got in her lap and then reached for Jamison.

"You don't love mom mom?" Leah said acting as if she were sad as she handed him to Jamison.

Leah looked at NuNu and NuNu stuck up her middle finger. Leah smirked. She knew her best friend was getting annoyed and she didn't care. She was going to make her wait just because she knew it would get up under her skin. She went back to talking to Jamison and NuNu stood. Before she could make her way to where Leah was sitting Tyson grabbed her by the arm.

"Hop up." He demanded.

His stare penetrated hers. NuNu looked at him and like always she felt an instant pulse begin between her thighs. She knew it was his way to stop her and Leah from going at it but now he had her on one and she was needing him to check the pressure she had building. She hopped up and wrapped her legs around his way. Tyson smacked her ass playfully. He hadn't got a chance to fill his lady because mother nature was hating like a muthafucka. So, while their son was occupied, he would take her upstairs and pipe her down because he knew she needed it just as much as he did.

"Y'all got y'all nephew, right?" Tyson asked as he started for the stairs.

He didn't even wait for them to respond. He knew they would keep an eye out on him. Tyson only asked to be courteous. He was kissing NuNu all in her mouth as his manhood started to grow inside of his jeans. Leah and Jamison peered at each other and shook their heads. Tyson and NuNu never had any shame in their game. They didn't care who was around when Tyson had a craving, NuNu fed it. Always fed it because if she didn't, she knew some other bopper around the city would. Tyson stayed trying to get hollered at and it worked NuNu nerves.

"We got him, with y'all nasty ass," Leah said smiling.

Tyson began to take heavy steps up the stairs. His dick was screaming for NuNu and the way she was grinding against the fabric of his jeans he knew she was ready.

"And we're having a boy, bia bia!" Leah called out.

"That explains why my baby don't like yo ass." NuNu shot back.

Chels laid across the living room floor of her parent's moderate home. She was thankful that they were overseas on vacation. She needed the time alone to heal and think without them breathing down her neck about her and Jamison's relationship. They were under the impression that he was the father of her baby. They had no clue that he hadn't fathered their first grandchild. A tear slid down her face as she reminisced on the days she and Jamison would lay in the middle of this same floor on the weekends and watch movies all day as teenagers. They were smitten with one another and Chels just knew that they would always be together. How had they gotten to this point? Chels shook her head and shame filled her.

She thought back on her childhood. The things she had endured caused her to become someone else. Chels thought back to the night when she was just 15, it was right before she met Jamison and her mother's brother had introduced her to sex. He made her feel things that she was always curious about. She had become strangely addicted to hearing how pretty she was and sex. Always wanting to chase the feeling that he had given her. Chels didn't realize that he had robbed her of her innocence. She simply looked at it as love and had been wanting it from any boy and now men who would give her that type of pleasure.

Chels had never told Jamison about what had happened to her. She never told anyone. She had allowed her uncle to use her body for the rest of the summer without anyone knowing and felt emptied once it was time for him to go back home. It was sick but Chels found something addicting in what he provided. Now here she was a grown woman with sex issues and chasing a feeling that she should have never experienced at the hands of a family member. Her life had always been hard and losing Jamison had made it worse.

Her phone buzzed next to her, snapping her out of her thoughts.

Marcus- You good?
Chels- Just leave me alone, I should have never told you about this fucking baby.
Marcus- Man, get off that. It is what it is. Neither of us wanted this but we have no choice but to deal with it.
Chels- Just leave me alone.

Chels silenced her phone and stood to her feet. Her shoulder was sore and the baby in her stomach had her lower back aching. Her feet were swollen, and her nose was huge. She didn't feel like herself. She took burdened steps to the lower level half bathroom. Chels stared in the mirror. The bags under her eyes looked like they were too heavy to even carry. She hadn't slept much since they released her from her 72 hours hold in the psychiatric ward at the hospital. She hadn't told anyone that Tyson shot her, she blamed it on herself and was committed after.

"Jamison." She cried out in agony.

Her heart ached, she wanted him so bad. She grabbed the medicine that she was prescribed off the sink and went back into the living room. Chels picked her phone up and went to Jamison's contact. She thought about calling him but knew he wouldn't answer. So instead of calling and letting her number show up

"I know he won't answer." She whispered.

She dialed *69 and called him private. She was sending silent wishes up in the air that he would answer. She held her breath as she listened to the phone ring twice before he picked up. Chels voice caught in her throat when she heard him say hello. *Should I speak*, she thought.

"JJ. Please forgive me and come…"
CLICK.

Chels looked down at the phone and her eyes instantly produced hot tears. She just wanted him to listen and he refused. She wanted her life back with him because living life without him was killing her each day. She wasn't used to not hearing his voice or not waking up next to him. She now knew what people meant when they said you never know what you have until it's gone. Jamison was gone and she was desperately trying to find her way back to him. She was yearning to be back in his life because he was the greatest love she had ever known.

He got me fucked up if he thinks we're not going to talk, she thought. Chels went to her bedroom and pulled out a white dress. It was the dress she had worn on her 21st birthday. Jamison's favorite dress. She slid the dress on, barely getting it on because of the growing belly and did her hair. Soft curls that fell passed her shoulders. She applied black lipstick and slid on heels. Chels grabbed her keys and headed out the door she was going to get her man yet again.

Chels drove to Jamison's house and parked the car. She noticed the lights on and climbed out the car. He had to be home if the lights were on. She walked up the driveway and knocked on the door. Like always she knew a way to get inside his home. She wasn't leaving until they talked. Just her and him, no one else. She climbed through the kitchen window. She slipped as she came down but caught herself.

"Shit."

Chels tiptoed around his home, she made her way up to his bedroom, their bedroom because in her mind it was still them. She went into his drawer and retrieved her normal sleepwear. His boxers and a white beater. When Chels closed the drawer, her heart sank. She reached out for the laminated photo. An ultrasound of Jamison's son. Her entire heart shattered when she read the name that was across the top of the sonogram.

"Noooo." She whined.

Chels swiped everything off the dresser. Pain shot through her shoulder, but she didn't care. The adrenaline that was coursing through her had her mind far from the pain in her shoulder because the ache in her chest hurt far worse. Her tears were uncontrollable. She knew this one thing, this one creation, had eliminated any chance they ever had. She knew it. He always wanted a family and Leah gave him just that. She had given him the very thing that Chels knew for certain had him locked in forever. A baby. A baby that was supposed to be his and hers. She looked down at her own growing belly and punched herself dead in it.

"Fucking hate you," She cried out.

"JJ nooo."

Snot and tears covered her face. Chels hit her stomach repeatedly.

"Aghhh." She said gritting her teeth.

I don't want to be here, she thought as she fell to the floor. A prescription bottle was in her line of sight. She reached for it and read the label. It was prescribed to Leah. A bottle full of Tylenol 3's that Leah never took because she didn't like how it made her feel. Chels opened emptied the entire bottle into her hand and hawked up saliva. She popped two of the pills into her mouth. He was never coming back to her and she knew it. She popped two more pills in her mouth and swallowed.

"He's never coming back." She cried.

Chels continued the process until the entire bottle was gone. She hawked up saliva and popped the pills in her mouth, swallowing them down with the fluids she hawked up. Chels raised from the floor and kicked off the heels she was wearing. She slid out of the dress and noticed blood. She didn't care. Chels knew she was miscarrying, or she had done damage, but her heart was damaged. She slid into Jamison's things and climbed right in his bed just as she used to and cut the T.V. on. Since she knew she could no longer have him, she didn't want to live without him. So, she would lay in his bed one last time before it all ended, leaving her first love her only love to be the one to find her.

CHAPTER 19

*L*eah watched as the city's lights of the night passed them by. She was grateful for the peaceful scene as they headed home. It had been a long day with the appointment, being at Tyson's, and then stopping home for sex and a nap. Now they were leaving dinner and she was tired. Pregnancy was starting to take over her body. She was always tired and always hungry. It hadn't been nothing like it was when she was pregnant with her daughter. Being pregnant with a boy had different effects on her body and Leah was already over it. She was wanting the next few months to fly by so that she could give birth to their son. She was grateful to be going through this pregnancy with someone she was sure wouldn't let her down. Leah looked over at Jamison, who was in a vibe as he nodded his head to *Dirt Off Your Shoulder* by Jay-Z. She gave a half smile as she watched him for a moment. That's when thoughts of what their son would look like crossed her mind.

She turned the radio down and Jamison looked at her.

"I'm sorry." She offered as she quickly turned the volume back up. Thoughts of Marcus crossed her mind, he hated for her to touch his radio and had smacked her one time when she did.

"You don't have to be sorry sweetie, what's up?" He asked as he turned the volume back down.

"Jamison, why did you choose me?" she quizzed.

It's not what she wanted to ask at first but thoughts of her past, was hunting her and she needed to know. She needed to know why he had chosen her, when he clearly still had someone that loved him. Jamison squinted as he looked at her and pulled over into the first parking lot he saw. He cut the engine off and turned to face her. *What did she mean why? Why the fuck wouldn't I?* He wanted to ask but he didn't let the words slip from his mouth. Leah twiddled her fingers as she waited for him to answer.

"Where did that question just come from?"

Leah shrugged.

"I just want to know." She said in a low tone.

Leah's voice was laced with something. Dipped in insecurity behind a clown ass nigga that had stripped her of her beauty. Marcus had robbed her of her worth because she no longer knew her value. Yes, she knew Jamison loved her, but Leah was just like any other girl. She got insecure sometimes and needed reassurance. Jamison never had to deal with this part of a woman. Chels had way too much confidence and it caused her to be a hoe. However, he knew he'd have to build that confidence back into Leah. He would have to replace what was stolen from her even though he wasn't the thief that took it.

"My heart chose you, Leah. The first day I ran into you, something was pulling me toward you, and I couldn't ignore it. Shit, it wouldn't let me. So, I'm giving my heart what it needs and that's you."

Leah's entire face warmed. *This fucking boy*, she thought. She leaned over the armrest and Jamison met her halfway and she kissed him. She gave his tongue a couple swirls of hers and then sucked on it before she pulled back. Jamison's dick went solid and Leah could see the monster bulging from his Ralph Lauren jeans.

"Get me home, baby," Leah whispered as she slid a finger inside her pants and then stuck that same finger in Jamison's mouth.

"Mmm." He groaned.

Jamison pulled his lip into his mouth, cut the car back on and peeled out the parking lot like a bat out of hell. He sped home. They were only ten minutes away, but it was like he couldn't get there fast enough. The way Leah's flavor melted on his tongue was like the butter that he used to flip pancakes. Now he was ready to flip Leah's cakes every which way because he had a hunger for her and only her cake would do. Jamison pulled in his driveway and frowned when he noticed Chels car. *What does she want now?* He thought.

Leah looked at Jamison and frowned.

"Um, who's car is that?" she asked looking from Jamison back toward the car.

"Chels." He said with a sigh.

Leah let out a sigh of her own. She didn't have time for this shit. Every time she turned around it was something with her. She just couldn't let go. Why couldn't she let go? *With the monster he got I probably wouldn't let go either*, Leah thought. Leah smirked at the thought and the smirk instantly turned into a frown. She was supposed to be taking that monster for a ride once they got home. *Should have went to my damn house*, she thought.

"Imma go see what she wants," Jamison announced as he climbed out of the car. He ducked his head back down into the car before he shut the door.

"Stay here."

Leah's face twisted up and she smacked her lips. She climbed out of the car anyway. Leah was annoyed and not only that but hard-headed. She did what she wanted to do.

She entered the house, kicked her shoes off and went straight upstairs. Leah peeled out her clothes and left them strewn all over the floor as she climbed the steps. Leah heard the T.V. playing when she reached the top step and was slightly muddled. She knew it wasn't on before they left. She walked down the hall. The bedroom door was wide opened and when Leah stepped in, she gasped in horror. Her hands flew to her mouth when she saw blood.

"Jamison!" Leah screamed as she backed away from the room.

Jamison heard Leah from the bottom step and ascended them two at a time. He was damn near running the way his long legs took to the steps. He saw Leah back against the wall and rushed to her.

"What's wrong sweetie?" he asked.

Leah's eyes were shut as she pointed towards the room.

"She. She. She's in the bed and there's blood everywhere." Leah muttered.

Jamison's eyebrows dipped and he turned toward the room. When he proceeded inside his stomach hollowed at the sight of Chels in his bed.

"Chels!" He screamed as he rushed to her.

"Leah, call 911!" He shouted.

Jamison looked down at Chels and he gritted his teeth letting out a guttural growl. He checked her chest to see if her heart was beating and then put a finger under her nose. She wasn't breathing.

"No. No. No." He said in a low tone.

He was trying his hardest not to break but tears were stinging his eyes.

"What did you do Chelly Chel."

Jamison was torn between scooping her up and leaving. He didn't want Leah to get the wrong idea but damn his moral compass was telling him to hold her. She had done this because of him. All she wanted was another chance and

Jamison had refused to give her that. He scanned her entire body and in her left hand, he noticed Leah's ultrasound picture in his hand. Jamison sighed as he closed his eyes and dropped his head. He now had his answer but why was she bleeding? *What the fuck did you do Chels?* He thought. Jamison scanned the room and noticed things all over the floor. His eyes landed on the empty pill bottle and his legs gave out from under him.

Leah entered the room and witnessed Jamison on the floor. She felt sorry for him in this moment. Leah couldn't imagine the thoughts that were going through his head right now. She took slow steps toward him, trying her hardest not to look toward the bed. She crossed the room and kneeled next to him.

"Are you okay baby?" she questioned as she wrapped her arms around his shoulders.

Jamison sniffed and nodded. Leah knew he was lying but she didn't say anything. How could he be okay?

"It's okay to feel baby, it would be selfish and wrong of me to expect you not to."

Jamison's chest tightened and a tear slid down his face. It was shit like this, that made him love Leah. It was her natural ability to be selfless when he needed her to be. She was truly a different breed and he knew because of her ability to be this way with him was the reason why she would forever be a part of his world.

"It's shit like that, that makes me love you more sweetie."

He kissed her and then they both stood once they heard sirens and heavy knocks at the door. He looked over to Chels one last time.

"Take a minute while I go get the door." Leah offered.

She made her way out the bedroom, with a heavy heart and tears of her own that finally released. They had had their differences but to be a witness to the scene in that room would make even the toughest man cry. A woman had taken her life and her child's life. *Marcus's child,* Leah thought. She shook her head and went to answer the door. She swiped at her face and cleared her throat.

"She's upstairs," Leah whispered as she pointed in the direction of the steps.

Leah watched as the paramedics made their way up the stairs. She shook her head in disbelief and then pulled out her phone to call her godmother. Leah needed her and she knew that Jamison would too. Leah went to dial her god mom's number and paused. She looked up toward the steps and then at the phone. She grabbed her keys off the key hook and left. Leah couldn't stay another minute in that house. She would give Jamison time to answer questions and be with his first love for the last time. She didn't know how she would comfort him after coming home to something so life changing. She couldn't fathom having to find Marcus in such a predicament. Her stomach twisted at just the thought. Leah made her departure and headed straight for Stacy's house.

Leah told her godmother the entire story and Stacy listened with her mouth agape while tears clung to her eyelashes. Ma'laysia carried short legs into the kitchen and reached for her mother. Leah smiled at her baby girl as she picked her up and sat her baby in her lap. She kissed the top of Ma'Laysia head and then buried her nose into the top of her daughter's head. A knock at the door pulled Stacy from her seat and she went to answer the door.

When Stacy returned to the kitchen this time, Tyson and NuNu were trailing behind her. Leah's tears spilled down her face when they walked in and she shook her head. She was overwhelmed with so many emotions coursing through her. Why couldn't she and Jamison just have a drama free life? Why was it constantly one thing after another? Leah could see if it were minor issues. This situation with Chels was extreme. She thought of Mandy and terror struck her. Memories of the day she had seen Mandy laying on the bathroom floor sent her into shock. Her breathing increased and her tears were uncontrollable. Stacy rushed to her.

"Calm down Bre'Ana," Stacy said.

Leah gripped her godmother's arm as she breathed hard and fast.

"Slow down baby, slow down. It's going to be okay. Don't stress you or this baby out." Stacy coached.

"Calm down boo," NuNu cut in.

Stacy pulled Leah to her feet and embraced her. She wrapped soothing arms around her daughter. Stacy began to rub Leah's back as she whispered in her ear.

"Shhh. It's okay, baby girl."

Leah took in a deep breath and released it slowly. The stuff she had endured over the last year and a half had been haunting and fearful. When would it get better? What had she done to deserve the trauma? It was like it had followed her since her childhood. She just wanted to be happy and raise a family with a man that was going to always put his family first. A man that was going to love her just as much as she loved him. She had Jamison but everything with him had been complicated and now this. She had to witness his ex-girlfriend take her life over her man. Her child's father. *Where is he?* She thought. It had been three hours and Leah hadn't heard a word from Jamison.

A heavy knock pulled Leah out of her thoughts.

"Ty, will you go get that for me?" Stacy asked.

Before the words left her mouth NuNu was already heading to the door. She pulled it open and Marcus stood at the door. NuNu looked him up and then down with one eyebrow raised. She couldn't stand this boy, never could and never would.

"What yo black ass want?" She spat.

Marcus smacked his lips and bit into his bottom lip. He was tired of her smart mouth ass always having something to say.

"Man, bitch."

The door flew open and Tyson had his gun drawn. One thing he didn't play was someone disrespecting his lady. Just because he was Leah's baby father, didn't mean he was exempt and Tyson was about to put hot led in his head about his. Shit about Leah too now that the opportunity was presenting itself.

"Yo, Ty man, no offense but she always got some slick shit to say. I'm going through enough shit right now." Marcus conceded with his hands raised.

Tyson stepped close. He was tired of extending passes to this nigga. However, he couldn't just pop the nigga and his god daughter was inside. Tyson pulled his bottom lip into his mouth. His nose flared as he weighed the options. He wasn't with letting this shit slide with Marcus any longer and if he didn't do something it would eat away at him. Tyson swiped a hand down his smooth face. *Fuck this shit.* Tyson quickly handed the pistol to NuNu and then pushed Marcus. Marcus stumbled slightly before catching his balance and then swung on Tyson. This silent beef between them had been simmering and Tyson was now turning it up to boil. Marcus had disrespected one too many times. Tyson leaned back missing the hit and sent two quick punches to Marcus chin and jaw.

"Tyson!" Stacy yelled.

The two boys stumbled off the porch and landed on the concrete. Tyson had the advantage landing on top and sent blows flying all over Marcus's face. Marcus grabbed Tyson by the waist and then flipped him over his head. Marcus quickly stood then kicked Tyson. He went to kick him again, but this time Tyson caught his foot and pulled him to the ground. He locked Marcus' head under his shoulder and punched him over and over. NuNu being NuNu smiled as she watched her man defend her.

"Ty!" Leah screamed as she came outside to the commotion.

"Lay is here."

Tyson couldn't hear a damn thing. He was going to show Marcus that disrespecting his lady would always come with a consequence.

"Nigga I told you I don't fucking play about her."

Tires screeching through the night's air caught everyone's attention. Everyone except Tyson because he had a point to prove. Jamison hopped out of the car and quickly ran up to the yard.

"Big Ty. Chill." Jamison barked.

"Let the nigga go."

Tyson sent one last punch to the back of Marcus' head and then released him. Leah and Stacy came off the porch.

"Ty you know better." Stacy chastised.

"When it comes to him respecting mine, I don't know nothing," he shot back.

"No disrespect G but this dummy had that shit coming."

"Chill Ty." Jamison said once more.

Marcus stood as Leah helped him up. Jamison looked in shock. *What the fuck is she doing?* He thought. Marcus was a grown ass man and no longer any of her concern. So why was she helping him?

"Leah this what you want?" Jamison asked.

Leah looked in confusion.

"What? No." She shot back.

"I just." She stammered.

"It looks like you just about to get this nigga shot out here if you don't stop playing nurse Leah. He good, he doesn't need your assistance sweetie." He stated with nothing, but finality in his tone.

Everyone's eyes rolled over to Jamison. He was the mutha

fucking nigga. He said what he meant and meant what he said. This would be his only time allowing Marcus to be this close to his future wife. He wasn't trying to be controlling because he wasn't that type. However, he would be respected and her helping her baby daddy up after a fight, he wasn't with it. That sentiment made him think that she still cared.

"Gone head bring your cute ass this way," Jamison said with a wave of his hand.

Leah strutted her cute ass right next to him. NuNu smiled. *These boys are crazy*, she thought.

"Nu, ain't shit funny bitch." Leah whispered.

Stacy looked at everyone pissed off once her grandbaby came to the screen door crying. She didn't play and the fact that they had drama going on in front of her house had her ready to whoop some ass.

"Leah and Jamison in the house now. Ty and NuNu y'all go the hell home so he can cool off. Marcus, you wait in the car for me to bring my baby to you."

Stacy spit them orders out as if she had been practicing saying them in her head. She was over the bullshit and right now she just needed to be able to talk to her kids and make sure they were okay after the things that had taken place.

"What I do G mommy?" NuNu quizzed.

"Girl, take you and your big head ass man home, sitting here smiling while he out her acting a monkey."

NuNu laughed and shook her head. She did as she was told when it came to Stacy. She and Tyson began to make their departure.

"Don't ever fucking disrespect her again," Tyson said in a low tone. They went to the car, NuNu being the driver and pulled off. Stacy shook her head. *They have lost their damn minds*, she thought. She marched Leah and Jamison right in the house and scooped Ma'Laysia up along the way. She kissed the top of the baby's head and rubbed her back. Stacy got her dressed and ready to go in ten minutes. She took Ma'Laysia outside to her father. Marcus assisted Stacy with getting his daughter settled in the car and then looked at Stacy.

"Thank you for calling me." Marcus said.

"No need to thank me. Go spend time with your daughter and get your mind off all this. You going to be okay?" She asked, looking at him.

Stacy could see the hurt in Marcus' eyes. His finding out about Chels had put something on him and she could tell. He had lost a child, so she had to empathize with that. She knew what it was like to lose a child. Stacy had felt like she lost Jamison the day she gave him up. It had taken her 25 years to finally get him and it was by chance that she had done so.

"I'm good," Marcus said.

"Stacy, I seen that ring on Leah's finger. Is she about to marry him?" Marcus asked.

Stacy nodded. Marcus closed his eyes and dropped his head in disbelief.

"She's moved on Marcus and you have too. I know this is a lot to deal with but don't ever disrespect anyone ever again when they are in my household, especially not mine," Stacy said giving him a warning look.

Marcus nodded. He wasn't trying to go back and forth with Leah's mom. He appreciated her because had it not been for her, he would have a hard time getting his daughter. Leah wanted nothing to do with him at all. He was surprised she extended a hand to help when he was down. Only if Marcus knew she was only doing it because she felt bad for him. Had he not got the news about Chels and their unborn baby, Marcus would have never even been a thought. He just wanted to talk to her. Hell, he wanted to be with her. Marcus missed Leah so much that he called her name in his sleep and would have to argue with Chrissy every morning that it happened about it. He just couldn't let go. Leah had been the only one to expose him to love and though he took her for granted he indeed did love her. Chrissy tried but she just wasn't the one he wanted. Marcus wanted the girl with the dope heart and soul. The girl with the aura that had captured him the first day he met her. His Leah. Now his Leah was planning to be someone's wife. Jamison had put a ring on her finger before Marcus could even get the chance to rectify his wrongs with her.

Stacy went to the back seat and pecked her granddaughter's nose and then closed the door. She patted the top of the car as Marcus started the engine and pulled off. She looked toward the house and shook her head. It was time for her to go in the house to make sure her two were okay.

$\mathcal{T}$yson and NuNu pulled in front of their home and sat in silence. NuNu leaned over the center console and kissed Tyson. She had been wanting to put her lips on him ever since he first pulled his gun out on Marcus. Seeing his anger always turned her on. She was used to getting his soft reserved side with a mannish mouth. However, when his other side came out, she loved it and now she was ready to bend that little shit over as Tyson would say. She stroked him through the fabric of his sweatpants, and he groaned. *God, I love him*, she thought.

She stroked him and he reached down in front of her pajama pants and massaged her sex through her panties. NuNu gave a little wind of her hips and let a low moan escape her lips. *Shit.*

"You going to let me pipe that lor shit down lor mama?" Tyson asked. His baritone was deep, and his Baltimore accent was heavy. NuNu didn't answer. She just kept winding her hips and moaning.

"Nu'Asia." Tyson groaned as he slid her panties to the side and put pressure on her swollen bud. NuNu let out a yelp and squirmed in her seat.

"Yes, daddy," She answered.

Tyson removed his hands from her pajamas and went to get out the car. He winced when he started to open the door. *Shit*, he thought. He pulled back his fist and noticed that it was swollen. *Fuck.* He shook off the pain and climbed out. He wasn't going to let it stop him from digging off in NuNu. She was soaked for him. Always soaked for him and she needed him to play janitor tonight and do some mopping because she was sending out wet signs through her moans.

They quickly entered the house and NuNu didn't even let him get in the door good. She hopped up on him, grinding her pelvis against him. She was ready, so ready that her womanhood ached for him. Tyson took long strides through the living room and straight up the stairs. It was nothing but kissing and moaning going on once they hit the bedroom. Tyson tossed NuNu on the bed and she came out of her shirt swiftly. She leaned back on her elbows as she watched him stand in front of her and come out of his shirt. His pants followed as he stood there with hard dick bulging from his boxers.

"Why them fucking pajamas still on?" he asked aggressively.

In one rapid motion, her pajama pants and panties were gone. NuNu laid back and put one finger in her mouth. She circled her tongue around it slow and seductively. She then slid it down her chin, to her chest, circled each breast and then down her stomach.

"Should I go further?" she whispered seductively.

Tyson pulled his lip into his mouth and rubbed a hand over his wavy head. He nodded and released his bottom lip. He smirked and then nodded again. NuNu closed her eyes and then slid that one finger down the center of her swollen sex. She released a moan when her finger entered her wet. Tyson sucked his teeth.

"Shit." He groaned.

Tyson slid out of his boxers as he watched NuNu please herself. Her moans sent sparks through him. He wanted to replace that finger with his throbbing man. He stroked himself watching his lady make love to her finger. NuNu opened her eyes and with one curl of a finger, she beckoned for him to come to her. Tyson wasted no time. He was on top of her in 2.2 seconds.

"You about to get Big Ty tonight lor mama."

He flipped her over swiftly and entered her from behind. NuNu's womanhood swallowed Tyson as he rammed in and out of her. Nice and slow. In and out. *Damn*, he thought as he looked down at the mess they were making. NuNu's arms were stretched above her head and she allowed the sheets to drown out her noises, burying her face deep into them. Tyson pulled her up.

"I want to hear you lor mama."

He hit that shit harder and NuNu gasped.

"Tyyyy," She squealed.

"Lay down."

Tyson pumped into her a few more times before withdrawing from her and laying on his back. NuNu reached on the nightstand and cut the radio on. The sounds of H-Town filled the room. Tyson and NuNu were definitely knocking boots.

She straddled him, reverse cowgirl style and took him on a ride. Tyson groaned and it only gassed NuNu's head up. She lifted both arms high above her head and rocked to the beat, going up and down. Tyson held onto her hips wincing from the pain in his hand as he assisted her, but she didn't need assistance. She had this bull ride down pack. NuNu's stomach muscles worked as she rolled her hips seductively. She didn't need to exercise. Tyson was the machine that she would use to get them abs back.

"Damn, lor mama work that shit. Fuck."

NuNu sped up and her head fell back as she felt herself about to release her sweet nectar all over him.

"Cum on this dick baby. Shit."

He knew she was close the way she was pulsing on him. Tyson thrusted up and NuNu climaxed all over him.

"Shit daddy." She cried out.

"Mmhmm." He offered.

NuNu's legs gave out on her and she fell back onto him. Tyson stayed in the same position and finished the job. Pumping in and out of her so he can join her on the high she was on. Tyson lifted her slightly so that he could see himself disappearing, in and out of her. The sight just did something to him. NuNu moaned and stiffened. Another orgasm.

"Let that shit go lor mama."

Tyson hit that shit one last time, hard before they both came simultaneously. He gave her one last pump making sure he emptied everything into her. He wanted another baby, another boy and was making sure he didn't waste a drop of what was needed to create one. The thought of a baby had Tyson wondering why she hadn't turned up pregnant yet. It took her no time to get pregnant with their son. Their son was a year old now and Tyson had been planting his seeds in her for the last few months.

He slid NuNu from off the top of him and she rolled over to face him.

"Lor mama."

"Huh," She called lazily, eyes closed. She was in the transition of being awake and asleep. Their sexual encounter had taken all of her energy and a dream was calling her name.

"Why haven't you got pregnant yet?" Tyson asked.

"I mean shit it took nothing for you to get pregnant with Baby Ty."

That question woke NuNu up and her heart began to race. Tyson sat up. He could see the bullshit all over her face. She was taking too long to respond and to Tyson, that meant one of two things. She was either about to lie or she had already lied. Before he would ever let a lie come between them, he would get the truth.

"Lor mama don't dare think about lying to me. Tell me straight up." He said.

NuNu raised from the bed and slid back into her clothes. She hadn't let one word come from her mouth and it only began to piss Tyson off.

"Nu'Asia." He barked.

"I don't want no more fucking kids Ty." She yelled as she turned to face him.

"Damn. Why do I have to stay pregnant, I do have shit I want to do in life and to be pregnant all the time is not one of them."

Her words knocked the wind out of Tyson. Here he was about to get upset when he hadn't considered what it was, she possibly wanted to do. He just assumed that he would be the only one in the house to take care of everything. How could he forget that she wanted to go to college for her master's degree? He wanted NuNu to be a housewife and raise his kids. Three at the most. Her words now had him feeling like shit, like a selfish ass nigga that wasn't aware of his own woman's wants. Tyson dropped his head and shook it. He raised from the bed and stood in front of her.

"I'm sorry lor mama."

NuNu stood there with her arms folded and her lips poked out. She looked like a pouting brat and it caused Tyson to smirk. He kissed her lips, her nose and then nudged it with his.

"You forgive me." He said as he pushed her toward the bed.

Tyson laid her down and snatched her pajamas back off. Her talking to him like that made his dick hard and now he was ready for round two. He huddled over her and slid into her.

"Agh." She cried.

Tyson kissed her lips.

"Next time talk to me baby. Tell me what you're thinking because your wants are important to me baby." He said as he pushed his throbbing man into her slowly.

Round two lasted longer than round one. Tyson was doing some making up. The sting of her not wanting more kids at the moment cut him slightly but he had to be selfless. They showered and then laid in bed. Tyson had the club and other things going on, so he was ready to hear what it was that NuNu wanted to do as far as going back to school. They laid and talked until NuNu dozed off in the middle of the conversation. Tyson kissed her forehead and whispered,

"I'm sorry lor mama."

He rolled over, tucking his good hand behind his head and stared up at the ceiling. It was time to start making moves. NuNu was ready to help him build an empire and the way she spoke let him know that she was ready to run a day to day business. He was going to send her back to school so that she could get her degree and then the takeover would begin. Her logic on waiting to extend their family made Tyson respect her much more. He couldn't wait to see her grow into the woman he knew she was destined to be the first day he took her to his home. Tyson had just got so caught up in his life he neglected his woman's dreams and for that he kicked himself. However, now that they had an understanding, he was sure that their life would soar to the highest level.

"Leah do I got to worry about you going back to your baby daddy," Jamison asked as they laid on Stacy's couch.

They were staying at her house for the night. He wouldn't be returning to his home. On the drive to Stacy's, he had already made up his mind to sell the house. He couldn't stay there; it had already begun to have an eerie feeling to it. They would officially begin to live in the house he bought Leah for her birthday. Jamison laid in back and Leah laid in front of him. He massaged her stomach as he spoke to her. He knew how the baby daddy and baby mama relationships went and now after everything that has been going on, he just wasn't with the games. So, he wanted to know straight up how it was.

"Hell no." She said a bit louder than intended to.

"I'm sorry about what happened. It was disrespectful and I promise to never disrespect you like that again baby."

Jamison kissed the back of her head and continued to rub her belly. He didn't say anything after that and that alarmed Leah. His silence made her begin to worry. *My dumbass*, she thought. Leah shook her head. She couldn't be mad at Jamison for thinking whatever it was he was thinking.

"Why you shaking your head sweetie?" He quizzed.

Leah turned to face him. She stared into brooding eyes and felt like she had hurt him with her actions.

"Does this make you feel different about me?" she whispered.

"Naw, sweetie. I told you before I know how it goes. I just want you to be sure this what you want." He said raising the hand that held his ring on it.

Jamison didn't want her to be indecisive. He didn't want the back and forth between the two men. She had to be his and his only because he wasn't with sharing. That was the reason why he and Chels didn't make it. He closed his eyes and shook his head. He was giving his all to this young girl. He didn't want to be made a fool of at the end. Jamison was giving Leah his all and in return he just wanted her to love him and be faithful. Leah's eyes misted.

"I'm sorry, baby and yes I'm sure. This is what I want."

Leah held the side of his face and stared in his eyes.

"You and the family we have made is it for me handsome man." She said, kissing his lips.

Jamison didn't need any further explanation. Her words held truth. She was sincere and that's all he wanted. That's all he needed was that reassurance because he didn't want them to raise their child separately, that's not what he wanted for his son. A two-parent home would do him justice. Society already had statistics about black families. They called them broken and that much was true, but Jamison wanted to be the man to prove the outsiders wrong. He wanted to be the man to raise a family with a wife and not a baby mama. There was a difference between the two and Leah was more suitable for the wife title. He was going to be the man to boss her life up because she deserved all the good that was coming her way. She had endured enough in life and he was going to be the one to make her feel something other than what she was used to. Another statistic that was placed upon the culture, that black men couldn't uplift their women. Jamison was that nigga, so he was making it his mission to be her protector, her provider and the man to love her unconditionally.

"I love you, sweetie."

Leah gave him a warm smile and kissed his lips.

"I love you, handsome man."

Jamison leaned down and whispered into her stomach.

"I love you too baby Jizzle."

Leah looked down and smacked her lips. *Did this boy just call my baby Jizzle?* She thought.

"Boy," Leah began.

"His name Jizzle." Jamison interrupted.

"You a damn lie and the truth ain't in you." Leah shot back.

Jamison hollered in laughter. His laugh caused Leah to laugh because that was something, she hadn't heard him do in a while. His life had been just as hard as hers lately and to see his smile reach his eyes warmed her inside. Jamison leaned back down and raised her shirt. He kissed her there tenderly and Leah smiled. She shook her head and rubbed his head, as she watched him interact with their son. This feeling he gave her was amazing. To be loved like this is what Leah had been waiting for, hell what she had been hoping for and she had found it in someone who had come into her life unexpectedly.

"Your mama a hater," Jamison whispered and then pecked her stomach.

Leah laid there caressing Jamison's head until she fell asleep. The last thing she heard was him telling the baby that he loved him. When Stacy walked in, they both were asleep, and she smiled as she leaned against the frame that separated the living room from the hallway. They were hers. One blood born and the other gifted to her because Leah was certainly a gift, a gift that had been chosen to bring her son back into her life through love. Life worked in mysterious ways, but Stacy was grateful.

"I love y'all." She whispered before turning back to retreat to her bedroom.

CHAPTER 21

*M*arcus, City, and Shan Shan sat at Chrissy's dining room table. They had a game of *Black-jack* going as they talked in hushed tones about their next lick. Chrissy didn't know everything about Marcus. He wasn't that comfortable letting her all the way into his business like that. When Leah asked about how he got his money, he offered her explanation without hesitation. However, when Chrissy asked, he told her to mind her business and not to worry about his. Marcus just could not shake Leah loose; despite the fact he had gotten into a relationship with Chrissy. She had given birth to his son and he still could not love her. Care for her, of course, but to love her, it just wasn't going to happen.

Marcus eyed his cards and then peered into the kitchen where Chrissy was standing over the stove making him dinner. She was doing everything she possibly could for him and to him, but Marcus was selfish because he was only doing the minimum to her and for her. Her phone buzzed and she grinned slightly. *The fuck she smiling at?* He thought.

"Marc," City called snapping Marcus out of his thoughts.

"What's good?" Marcus asked.

City looked at Shan Shan and then back to Marcus.

"So, we going to push down on that nigga Tyson or what?" He asked in a hushed tone.

Marcus trained his eyes on his cards and then nodded. It was no way he was going to let the shit Tyson had done a week ago slide. Marcus never went anywhere strapped. He didn't want to get caught riding with it. Carrying a concealed weapon that wasn't registered was a sure way to get him sent to prison. He was tired of NuNu's mouth. Tired all of them muthafuckas and if Leah's new nigga wanted that work, he was prepared to give him some too.

"What about Leah's new nigga?" City quizzed.

"We going to make the move as well?"

Again, Marcus nodded. Hearing City say, *new nigga* sent a shock of pain to his heart. Marcus never thought he'd see that day Leah truly move on and be someone's first priority. She was giving another man the family that should have been his and his only. The womb that was finally starting to heal just a little bit was reopened and began to bleed out. *Damn*, he thought. Marcus slammed the cards down and stood. He hadn't spoken to Leah since the night it came out. Married. His first love was about to marry someone else and he didn't know how to feel. He just wanted to talk to her. Marcus needed her but it was clear that she wasn't coming back to him and that realization stung. He had lost her, lost her to another nigga. One that he once assumed was a rebound but evidence of the love she had for Jamison that night in Stacy's yard was present.

"What y'all niggas about to do, man?" Marcus asked.

Shan Shan and City already knew what time it was. Marcus didn't have to say anything else. They both laid their cards down and stood from the table. Conversation was over. Shan Shan walked up to Marcus and gave him dap. City followed behind him doing the same thing. They both knew that Leah was still a soft spot for him, and the mere mention of her name changed his mood. The boys stopped at the door.

"Get at us." Shan Shan said.

"Fa sho." Marcus countered.

Shan Shan and City made their departure and Marcus made his way to the kitchen. Chrissy was making plates when he walked in.

"Who got you cheesing so hard?" Marcus asked as he went to reach for her phone.

Chrissy quickly swiped it up from the counter.

"See, what we not going to do is check phones and shit. I don't go through yours, so I want the same respect playboy."

Marcus looked at her as if she were crazy. *Who the fuck she thinks she talking to?* He thought. The same look Marcus gave Chrissy, she politely returned it. She was tired of his bullshit. He had been walking around her house moping ever since he found out Leah was engaged. She loved him and wanted him but her patience for him to finally be what she deserved was weathering away. She had given this boy a family and the only one he could seem to think about is the one that didn't exist with Leah. Marcus had used her as a rebound. Using her as an attempt to get over his first baby mother. Chrissy was fed up and now was at the point that if he was going to be doing him, she would surely be doing her. Two were going to play that game.

"Man Chris, don't fucking play with me," Marcus warned.

"No, don't fucking play with me!" She yelled.

"I'm tired of your shit. Tired of catering to you. Tired of being your doormat. Tired of you acting as if me and my fucking son is your step kids. You praise the fuck out of Leah and y'all daughter. Talk about them like they are the best thing that has happened to you. Did you fucking forget MarKest is your son? Did you forget that I'm the girl that gave you a fucking son!"

"One that I didn't even want," Marcus shouted.

SLAP.

Marcus' head snapped to the right and as soon as the words flew out of his mouth, he regretted them. He closed his eyes and shook his head. Chrissy's entire heart dropped to the bottom of her stomach. Her gut hollowed and lip quivered. Her breathing became labored as her nose flared. How could he not want her baby? How could he even let something like that come out of his mouth? Chrissy stared at him. Her words were caught in her throat and the tears that she was trying her hardest to keep from falling, clung to her eyelashes.

"Chris. I'm sorry baby."

Chrissy shook her head. She stormed past him, bumping him on the way out. Marcus tried to stop her but failed at his attempt.

"Chrissy." Marcus barked.

"Get the fuck out!" She yelled.

"I'm sorry baby." Marcus barked back.

"I didn't mean that shit. I love my little dude man."

Marcus invaded Chrissy's space. He tried to get her to look at him, but she was not having it. He went to grab her chin and she maneuvered out of his grasp. Marcus tried again and this time Chrissy conceded. She turned her face to him slowly and when their eyes connected, she broke down. *How the fuck could he not want my son?* She thought. She just wanted him to treat them equally. Why did she feel like she was competing for a spot that Leah clearly did not want?

"That shit hurts. MarKest didn't ask to be here, I know and I'm not Leah but I'm here. Fighting and crying for love that she doesn't want. You should have just left me alone. You should have just let me go. But no, you came calling my phone every time she pissed you off or when she was at home at not with you or while she was at work. You called me and now you sit in my fucking house and tell me you didn't want my son." She cried as she pointed to her chest.

"That shit hurts."

"I didn't mean it, Chris. I swear. I'm sorry baby." He said kissing the top of her head.

MarKest began to whine and Chrissy snatched away from Marcus to go get her son. His words would forever ring in her ears. Chrissy crossed the room and picked their baby up.

"It's okay, baby," Chrissy whispered as she bounced him slightly and patted his back. She glanced at Marcus and could tell that he was sorry, she could see the remorse, but she didn't care, his words could never be unsaid.

"Leave Marcus." She said calmly.

Marcus placed his hands on, top of his head. He stared at her as she rocked their son back to sleep. He loved both of his kids. One wasn't more special than the other because they both come from him. Even though they had different mothers he still loved them both the same, he just never wanted them with no one outside of Leah.

"I'm not leaving baby, put him back to sleep and come talk to me." He said.

Marcus walked away and headed for her bedroom. He had to make this right. He was starting to develop something for her. He wasn't sure what it was but to see her hurt had hurt him. To see her cry caused him to tear up. However, even with all that, he still wanted Leah. It was just something about her that he couldn't let go of. Marcus wanted to text her. He had an urge to just tell her he still loved her. He went back and forth with himself before finally pulling out his phone and sending her a text.

Marcus- I love you Leah. Don't marry him please bey.

Marcus waited for a minute to see if she would text back. His heart dropped when she sent him a message back. He looked at the phone and closed his eyes. He was scared to even open the message. Marcus let out a sharp breath and clicked on her message.

Leah- And I love and will marry Jamison. Bye.

Marcus shook his head. *I'm going to fuck this bitch up man*, he thought.

Marcus- Fuck you and that nigga.
Leah- I just fucked him. That muthafuckn monster got me tired and he ain't gay so you can't fuck him with yo gay ass.

Marcus stood from the bed and went to grab his keys. When he snatched them off the table, Chrissy walked in the room. Marcus paused and looked at her. She stood there naked. Marcus licked his full chocolate lips and sat his keys back down along with his phone. He began to walk over to her but halted. Leah's message began to bother him. Just knowing that she was being intimate with someone else sickened him. His erection immediately went away and he shook his head.

"I'm not in the mood for this. I'm about to roll out." He stated. Marcus went back over to the table to retrieve his things and Chrissy scoffed.

I'm so sick of this shit, she thought. She quickly slid on clothes and went back to the living room where Marcus was holding their son. When she walked in Marcus looked up at her with sympathetic eyes. His words were haunting him because he truly did love their son.

"I'm sorry again Chris."

Chrissy ignored his apology. She had questions. When she tried to make him leave not too long ago, he would not and now all of a sudden, he was needing to leave.

"Where you going, Marcus?" She asked with her hand on her hip.

"I got shit to do." He said pecking the top of his son's head and then giving his little fist a pound.

Chrissy shook her head. *He always talking about he got shit to do.* Marcus handed her the baby and left without another word. *This nigga got me messed up,* she thought.

"I'm going to find someone to love me just like your other baby mama did!" She shouted.

Marcus pulled up to a house down from Leah's house and cut his car off. He had found out where she lived because he had followed her one day from Stacy's house. He had just dropped their daughter off to her and left her cup in the car when he circled the block Leah's car was pulling off from the house and he just trailed her. Knowing that Jamison had to be the one to purchase the home for her put him in a mood. Jamison was upgrading her life. Showing her that there were still men around and would have her living the life she was deserving of. It sickened him to know that she had moved on because he once was able to control the girl inside. He once had her heart but now those days were long gone. Marcus thought it was something still there that night in front of her god mom's house. The way she was showing she cared had him feeling like there was still hope. Only for him to find out she was about to get married. He was incognizant that not only was she going to be married but she was also getting ready to have a baby outside of their daughter.

If Marcus found out that she was pregnant that would be the very thing to make him snap. He could deal with knowing she was engaged because the way he looked at it, anything could happen, and she wouldn't get married. He was content with that but what he wouldn't be content with is knowing that she was going to give birth to Jamison's son. A son that he wanted to be the one to give her. Marcus didn't even bother to call or text before getting out of the car. He strolled up the long walkway, taking in the scenery around him. Jamison had her living nice and Marcus couldn't help but feel a bit jealous that this man had been the one to pull his baby mother.

He knocked on the door. He could hear Leah laughing as if she were talking on the phone. Marcus knocked harder this time. Leah's laughing seized and when she snatched open the door in nothing, but Jamison's boxers and a tank top Marcus froze. His heart plummeted when he saw her swollen belly. She was 29 weeks pregnant and had gone the whole 29 without him knowing. His eyes misted and anger took over him. Leah stared at him and recognized the look of rage in him. She had seen that look before. He looked the same way each time he had laid hands on her. Leah dropped the phone and tried to close the door. Marcus rammed the door with his shoulder and knocked Leah down. She scrambled to get up and took off for her bedroom where Jamison kept his extra phone. She ran but before she could even get halfway up the steps Marcus caught her and dragged her down the steps.

"You having this nigga baby?" He barked.

Leah's head hit each step and she cried out in pain. She tried kicking but she could no longer feel her legs. Terror overcame her as she gripped her stomach trying her best to protect hitting it in any kind of way. The last thing she wanted to do was lose her child. She would be crushed, and she knew Jamison would be devastated. This was his first child and Leah just couldn't lose his first child. She would never forgive herself.

"Marcus, stop!" She screamed.

"I can't feel my legs."

"Bitch shut the fuck up!" he yelled as he pulled her to the closest couch completely ignoring her cries.

"Help!" Leah cried.

When they made it to the living room Marcus dropped Leah's legs, pulled down the boxers she was wearing and pulled his sweats halfway down.

Leah's eyes widened and she screamed.

"Marcus please no, don't."

She knew what he was getting ready to do and she tried again to move but couldn't.

"Marcus please don't." She was begging now.

Marcus sneered and entered her womanhood. Rape. He was violating the mother of his child. He let out a moan as he thrusted in and out of her. Leah couldn't believe what was happening. She tried her best to fight him off her, but it was no use, she couldn't move her legs and the pain shooting through her head and back was becoming unbearable. She laid there crying as he had his way with her.

"You said I couldn't fuck you right?" he growled.

"I told you, you were mine."

Leah just laid there, calling for Jamison in her head as she closed her eyes because she could no longer let words escape her lips. Marcus pumped in and out of her furiously. He came inside her within minutes. It was then that he realized that she had closed her eyes. That's when he snapped out of the rage as if someone had said earth to Marcus. *What the fuck did I just do?* He thought. He pulled out of her.

"Leah." He called.

No response. He smacked her face. Nothing. Fear struck him and he began to panic. He looked around frantically. Tears began to form and there was nothing he could do but allow them to fall. Marcus was skating on a very thin line of insanity. He lost all logic when he noticed her stomach and acted out of pure emotional rage.

"Leah!" He shouted.

"Get up baby. Please get up."

Marcus rushed to the front door to close it and then ran back to Leah. He pulled out his phone and kneeled by her side. He began to dial 911 but paused. *What if she's dead, I'm going to jail*, he thought.

Marcus heard the locks on the door turning and stood quickly. *Shit.* He looked around and ran to the kitchen trying to find an exit. He slid out of the backdoor unnoticed and ran.

Jamison entered and noticed Leah's legs on the floor, but something was off. Normally when he walked in, she always greeted him. *What the hell she doing on the floor?* He thought. and she was just up. When he left, she had been on the phone with NuNu. Jamison walked further in the house.

"Sweetie."

Leah didn't respond. That's when he noticed the boxers and then her lying there exposed and not responding.

"Leah!"

CHAPTER 22

*J*amison stood looking in the window of the NICU where all the babies were. He stared at them all as a tear slid down his face. Babies didn't deserve to be enduring such things this early in life. What had they ever done? They deserved to come into this world healthy with zero complications. Why couldn't his son be one of those babies came into this world like that? Jamison stared at a handsome little boy who was nothing but 3lbs and 7oz. Jamison Semaj Banks Jr. His Jizzle. He and Leah's son had come into this world prematurely, but he was going to make it. Their son was a spitting image of Jamison. Jamison noticed his lips on his son right away. That was his trademark. Jamison shook his head because Leah hadn't got the chance to hold or kiss their son. He watched his baby boy's little chest rise and fall with machines helping him breathe as he sucked on his finger like he was still in the womb. *My Jizzle*, he thought.

Tyson approached Jamison and put a hand on his shoulder as he looked through the glass window. His nephew was a soldier already and it caused Tyson to smile. He knew he was going to be good, but the thought of Leah pained him. His sister had suffered during the rape and then the surgery of bringing her son into this world. Neither boys said a word. They just stood there watching the sleeping baby boy. They both had all types of thoughts running through their mind. Murder in particular. They didn't know who had done the thing that caused this chain of events, but they would be finding out if it was the last thing they did. NuNu had heard the commotion but wasn't able to make out what was going on. She had hung up and called Tyson and then the police. The police and ambulance had arrived a minute after Jamison had discovered Leah.

"You good, JJ?" Tyson asked.

Jamison sniffed. Hell no, he wasn't good. The birth of his son was supposed to be one of the best days of his life. Though he was grateful he was here, it hurt to know that he had suffered to be here. His baby boy almost didn't make it but pulled through. Jamison had never prayed so hard in his life but to make sure his baby made it, he prayed harder than ever.

"Naw, dummy I'm not good." He said in a low tone.

"Jizzle not breathing on his own and he can't be with his mama. That shit killing me."

Jamison shook his head.

"A nigga raped my heart and now my baby laying in a bed paralyzed and unconscious."

Jamison turned and buckled. He allowed his back to slap against the glass and slid down the wall. He brought his long legs up toward his chest and draped his hands over his head. Jamison's entire chest rocked as he cried. He had experienced a lot of heartache before, but this type of ache was different. The two people he loved more than anything was laying in the hospital because he wasn't around to protect them. When he said a nigga had raped his heart, he meant every word. He felt like he had been violated but he knew it couldn't compare to what he knew Leah felt in that moment and how she was feeling now. Jamison felt so guilty that once his son was born, he had left her room and been at his son's side. He couldn't even bring himself to look at her.

"My fucking baby needed me, and I wasn't there."

Jamison said it so low that Tyson barely heard him. Tyson was trying his hardest to be strong. Everyone was an emotional mess. NuNu, Stacy, and Jamison. So, Tyson was fighting within himself to be everyone's strength. However, his grief was beginning to take over the more and more Jamison spoke. He knew that feeling because at one point he too felt that he hadn't protected her. Tyson's guilt began to weigh on him and he had to sniff back emotions.

The elevator doors opened, and Stacy walked out of them. Her eyes were red and puffy, accompanied by a red nose from all the crying she had been doing. Tyson looked at her with sympathy. She approached the boys and when Jamison laid eyes on her he stood to his feet. They stared at each other for a moment before he finally broke.

"Ma." He called out.

Jamison fell into Stacy's arms. The word ma came out so freely that it touched both Stacy and Tyson's heart. She knew it was because of the moment that he had called her ma, but she still embraced him. Appreciating the thought of him needing her at the moment. She wrapped her short arms around him as he laid his head on her shoulder and cried.

"Shhh." She said soothingly.

"It's okay JJ."

Jamison shook his head. It wasn't okay. The fact that the love of his life was laying in the hospital for such trauma wasn't okay. His son. His son was born prematurely and that wasn't okay.

"I failed her. I was supposed to protect her, and I wasn't there when she needed me to be." He whispered.

Stacy rubbed his back as they rocked back and forth. Her son who had found his way to her by chance was the man she knew he would be. He and Leah's story would be beautiful because of the way they came together. They were going through rough times, but she knew that they would overcome them. Leah was going to be fine. Stacy was sure of it.

"You have to go to her JJ. Let her hear your voice. Go talk to her."

"I can't."

Jamison's words were caught in his throat. He couldn't even finish his sentence. Stacy sniffed and kissed the side of his cheek. It stirred something in Jamison. It was motherly and right now he knew he needed this from her.

"You have to. You have to go be there for her. Don't abandon her now, not when she needs you the most." She said.

"Look at me."

Jamison lifted from her shoulder slowly and wiped at his face. He released a deep breath as he peered down at her.

"You have to be strong for her and him," Stacy said nodding toward the NICU.

"They both need you JJ. They're your family. So, you have to be there for both of them. It will all be fine. Trust me."

Jamison sniffed and nodded. He knew Stacy was right. Leah was his future wife and he couldn't just not be there for her, despite the guilt he felt behind what happened to her. He knew he had to put his own hurt to the side and think about her and their son. They both needed him, and he was the man. He was their protector. So, from this moment forward he vowed to do just that. He would make sure they were safe, at all times and that something like this never happened again.

"You're right." He stated in a low tone.

He kissed Stacy's cheek and then headed back toward the glass window. He stared at his son for a moment before turning back to face Tyson and Stacy who were both looking at him. Jamison turned toward the glass one last time.

"Let me go check on mommy Jizzle. I'll let her know you said you love her."

Stacy smiled at her son. *Him and this damn Jizzle stuff*, she thought. When he turned back around, he noticed Stacy's smile and it caused him to give up a half smile. Jamison walked toward them and stopped right in front of Stacy.

"Go be by her side." She whispered.

"I'll sit here with Jizzle."

Jamison smirked and Tyson laughed.

"Send Nu'Asia crybaby ass down here. I'm going to sit and talk with G for a little bit." Tyson said.

Jamison slapped hands with Tyson and hugged Stacy before making his way to the elevators to go check on Leah. He stepped on the elevators and stared straight ahead as his mind raced. He didn't know why but he had a gut feeling that he knew who had done this. It was like it was man's intuition and he could sense that the person who did this to Leah was someone close to her. Jamison was going to make sure his family was fine before he retaliated. He didn't want anyone to think for one second that he wasn't going to come back and flip the city upside down to find who violated his woman.

NuNu sat at Leah's bedside, resting her head at the foot of the bed while she slept. It had been almost a whole 48 hours, and Leah still had not woken. The doctor had told them that she had suffered from a prolapsed disc. She was paralyzed temporarily and would need extreme physical therapy in order to get her mobility back. Hearing the news had broken everyone's heart. Leah was supposed to be enjoying her new bundle of joy. Instead she was laying in the hospital bed enduring yet again trauma.

The door creaked open and Jamison poked his head in. The sight of Leah laying there non-responsive injured him all over again. He closed his eyes and his chest tightened. *Oh sweetie,* he thought. Jamison stepped in the room and couldn't take his eyes off Leah. He looked at NuNu then walked further into the room. He walked up on her and nudged her awake. NuNu groaned as she opened her eyes to see Jamison standing in front of her. She lifted her head from the bed and wiped at the sides of her mouth.

"Ty want you, he said bring your cry baby, big head, nosey short ass downstairs." Jamison lied by adding his own little twist to Tyson's words. NuNu looked at him, smacked her lips and then laughed.

"He did not say all of that." She said, shaking her.

She stood and stretched her arms above her head. NuNu walked to the head of the bed and kissed Leah's cheek.

"Love you Leah boo." She whispered.

NuNu pushed Jamison as she walked out and chuckled. When she was out of the room, he took timid steps toward the bed. Jamison's eyes betrayed him as he studied Leah's entire body. He leaned in and kissed her lips gently like he was scared if he pressed too hard, he would hurt her.

"I'm sorry baby." He whispered lips still pressed to hers.

Jamison pulled a chair to the head of the bed and sat there. He grabbed Leah by the hand and kissed it letting hot tears roll down his face and onto her hand. He used this thumb to clear it from her hand and placed a delicate kiss to the spot where his tears had fallen. He began to envision their son laying in her arms while he looked at them in adoration. This was supposed to be a joyous moment for them both. He was supposed to be kissing her forehead right now, telling her how proud of her he is. Telling her thank you for bringing his son into the world. Not this. Not sitting next to her crying and praying for her to wake up soon.

Jamison lowered the bed rail so that he could get closer to her. He just wanted to hold her, but he was afraid to move her. He grabbed another chair that was sitting in the corner of the room and placed it in front of the one he was sitting in. Jamison stretched his legs out and placed size 12 feet in the chair. He laid his head on Leah's shoulder and held her hand.

"Jizzle said he loves you sweetie," Jamison whispered.

"He said that you are the strongest woman he knows and that since you're so strong that he will be strong."

Jamison's heart ached as he said the words. He shook his head. This just wasn't a way his family should be celebrating new life. He battled with himself about just leaving and allowing someone else to come up and be with her. Jamison's guilt was weighing on him heavily. The person behind the offense was also pressing down on him. He did not know why but his gut was telling him that Marcus had done this. His mind pandered since he found her laying on the living room floor. Nothing was taken. He didn't have anyone wanting to get back at him for anything. Jamison was solid and respected. Nigga's had no beef with him, so the only person he could think of was Marcus. He looked at her. *How could a nigga rape his own baby mama?* Jamison thought. Jamison didn't have proof that it was Marcus, but he was already charged in his head. That's when it hit him. The brown Regal that was parked a house down from Leah's house. He knew it was Marcus' car. He was the only nigga he knew in the city with a brown Regal. He shook his head and the color of his skin went red. *I'm going to murder that nigga.*

"Wake up for me baby," Jamison said in a low tone.

"We need you."

Jamison yawned and laid his head back on her shoulder, he was tired and hadn't slept since they arrived at the hospital almost two days ago. When Leah had come out of surgery, he went straight to NICU to be with his son. He had allowed Stacy and NuNu to sit upstairs with her while she went through another surgery for her back. He knew that their journey ahead was going to be rough. He had to prepare himself mentally for how he would need to be with her. Jamison had some choices to make. He had promised her that he would leave the streets alone to focus on his family and the legit business he ran. However, he would have to get Marcus out the way. There was no way he was going to allow him to breathe too much longer for the disrespect. Jamison was going to handle it personally. It pained him to know that he would be leaving Leah's daughter fatherless but shit he almost left him without a child. He couldn't let that slide. He would fill that void in Ma'Laysia's life, he had no problem with that. They already had a bond. She was his LayBay so she would always be good.

Jamison dosed off and when he woke up Leah wasn't in the room. He looked around slightly confused because he didn't remember falling asleep. He checked his phone and when he looked up, he noticed the door opening. He stood and rushed to the door. He snatched it open so fast that he startled the nurse that was wheeling Leah's bed back into the room.

"Has she woken up?" he asked.

The nurse looked at him and shook her head.

"We only took her for x-rays of her back. She didn't wake up during that." The nurse informed.

Jamison assisted her with putting Leah's bed back in its original spot. She locked the breaks on her bed and grabbed her chart from the bed. She checked the name on the chart against the name on Leah's wristband. Jamison watched as the nurse lifted the covers at Leah's feet to check for feeling and to see if she would respond. Jamison said a silent prayer in his head. He was hoping that she would move, even if it was just a little. Nothing. The nurse went to the other foot, repeating the steps. Again, nothing. Jamison shook off the sting of not getting a reaction. He knew that it probably wasn't going to happen, but it still didn't stop him from hoping and wishing for a positive outcome. The nurse pulled the cover back over Leah's feet and made sure she was comfortable before leaving the room.

When she finally left them alone, he sat down next to her and took her by the hand. He cupped her hand inside both of his hands and brought it to his lips. He just wanted her to wake up. He had to see her open those pretty eyes. He wanted to see her smile for him. Jamison would give anything to see Leah's dimple form in the top right corner of her mouth. He smiled at just the thought. He leaned over and kissed her lips.

"I love you, sweetie," He whispered.

"I'm about to go check on Jizzle. I miss him. I'll be back."

Jamison sent Stacy a message to come take over with sitting with Leah, while he sat in the NICU to visit his baby boy. He hadn't seen his face in almost 24 hours and he missed him terribly. Within ten minutes Stacy was walking in the room. Jamison hugged her and then bent down to kiss Leah once more before leaving to go to his son.

CHAPTER 23

FIVE WEEKS LATER...

*T*he house was silent and the sun was shining brightly through Leah's old room. It was early morning and the birds were chirping as Leah sat in bed holding her sleeping son. He was still small but, so handsome and Leah was in love. She was staring at a tiny duplicate of Jamison and she couldn't be happier that he had survived the trauma that she had endured. She just knew that he wasn't going to make it, but when she finally opened her eyes and was able to speak Jamison Jr was the first person she asked for. She had to know if he was okay and to lay eyes on him. When she laid eyes on him Leah couldn't do anything but cry. Her love child had survived. He was now her miracle baby because there was no way he should have made it. Leah stared at her son and let tears rain down her face.

"I'm so sorry baby." She whispered as she kissed his tiny little hands.

They had been home not even a full week and adjusting to life had been hard. The change had been overwhelming for everyone, but they were managing as best as they could. Leah hadn't wanted to go home and had been staying back at Stacy's since being released from the hospital. She had to have a medical bed replace her old one and a wheelchair for mobility. The thought of not being able to walk sickened Leah. She felt as if it was meant for her to suffer all her life because that's all she had been doing is suffering. It was like as soon as she felt even a little bit of happiness something traumatic came along and snatched it away. Like she had, *I love pain* written on her forehead.

A soft knock at the door pulled her from her thoughts.

"Come in." She said as quietly as possible. Leah didn't want to disturb Jamison Jr. She felt like his little ears were too sensitive for loud noise, so Leah did everything quietly these days.

Jamison peeked his head in. Leah peered up at him.

"Don't just stand there, handsome man.

Handsome man. The two words that always touched him behind his ribs. He entered and smiled instantly at the sight of them. His most valuable people in the world were home. Jamison took long wide steps to get to her bed. He slipped out of his shoes and slid in the bed next to her. He leaned his head on her shoulder and just watched as his son slept. Leah leaned into him and kissed the top of his head. Her boys. The only one that was missing was Ma'Laysia. She had been back and forth with NuNu and Tyson. They had taken on the responsibility of helping with her until Leah and Jamison were settled well enough with the new baby.

Leah missed her baby girl and would give anything to hear her running down the hall calling for her granny. Her birthday had passed, and Leah hadn't been able to throw her baby a birthday party. However, Stacy had made sure that her baby's first birthday had been successful enough and made sure she took lots of pictures for Leah to be able to see. She was grateful for that, but she had much rather she was home to see her daughter on her first birthday.

Jamison lifted his head from her shoulder.

"Give me Jizzle," Jamison ordered as he reached for him.

Leah smacked her lips and rolled her eyes.

"Stop calling my baby that. You not about to have him going to school telling people his name Jizzle." Leah said talking shit as she handed Jamison the baby.

"His name Jizzle sweetie, everyone calls him Jizzle but you. Get with the program."

Leah craned her neck back and stared at him.

"Boy his name is J Jr!" She exclaimed.

"Yeah J Jizzle." Jamison shot back.

He nuzzled his nose against the baby's and then kissed his forehead. Jamison looked at Leah and kissed her lips.

"He's a perfect blend of us sweetie. Thank you for giving me him."

Leah smiled and went to sit up in the bed and it was like a dark cloud appeared over her head. She gave herself a reality check that she couldn't move as freely as she used to. Leah would find herself lying in bed at night crying herself to sleep as she tried her hardest to get her legs to move. What good would she be if she couldn't walk? How could she properly take care of her kids? Could she even please her man? These things jumped around in Leah's mind daily as she tried to adjust to being immobile. However, she could not. She just could not ever get used to not being able to walk.

Leah sniffed as emotions began to overcome her. Jamison laid glossy eyes on her because he felt her turmoil. Leah stared at him. She felt like he was too good for her like he deserved someone much better. A woman that would be able to cater to him, make love to him, and who was whole. Not someone that was paralyzed and mentally damaged. Not someone who was scared to close her eyes at night because her first baby's daddy's imaged lived behind her eyelids when she did. When Leah would sleep, she would wake up in a cold sweat from the nightmares. Jamison deserved better and the thought of him leaving her one day made her sick to her stomach.

"Jamison, you're going to leave, aren't you?" Leah asked.

"Not fucking ever will I leave you." He shot back without thinking twice.

Leah whimpered.

"So, you're going to stay with me knowing I can't walk?"

Jamison shook his head.

"Leah. You not being able to walk isn't permanent baby. With therapy and hard work, you will get your mobility back. So no I'm not leaving you, I'd be a bitch ass nigga to leave you just because of that. That would only mean I never fucked with you anyway if I did that, like I was with you just because you got a pretty face and because you could walk." Jamison shook his head once more and then kissed his son again before finishing what he was saying.

"You're my forever Leah. You've given me the best gift anyone could have given me and to get rid of you would be nothing but disrespect to Jizzle. You're his mama and I could never in my fucking life disregard you like that."

"You bet the fuck not." NuNu said as she walked in the door hearing the last part of the conversation.

"Cause she got a sister that likes to fight."

Tyson walked in behind NuNu with Ma'Laysia on his back, shaking his head.

"Nu'Asia shut yo ass up. Why you always in somebody business lor mama damn."

Leah laughed and wiped her face.

"What's up LayBay," Jamison said, smiling at her.

"Mommy's Lay." Leah squealed.

Tyson walked across the room and Leah reached out for her baby girl. Tyson handed Leah her daughter and she pulled her in close and hugged her tightly. Leah planted kisses all over her daughter. Leah was just thinking about how much she missed her and it was as if Tyson and NuNu knew this is what she needed to help clear the dark clouds from the room.

"What y'all doing here so early in the morning?" Leah asked.

"Lay little ass kept calling for you when she first woke up, so we brought her to see her mama for a few." NuNu said as she kissed Jamison Jr hand.

"Hi god mommy Jizzle." She called out.

Tyson and Jamison looked at Leah and laughed. They knew she couldn't stand that name. Leah sucked her teeth and then rolled her eyes as she focused her attention back on Ma'Laysia.

"I told you to get with the program, sweetie," Jamison said jokingly.

Another knock at the door jarred everyone's attention to it. Stacy walked in and Eugene followed behind her. Leah beamed when she saw her father. Ma'Laysia was out of her arms in no time and ran to Stacy. Her favorite person. Leah smiled as she watched her baby girl run to Stacy. Eugene walked in the room and all eyes were on him as he made his way to the bed.

"My boy Jizzle."

Everyone in the room burst into laughter. Everyone except Leah. She didn't find it funny. Jamison looked at her smiling and Leah looked at him, shooting him a look that spoke words she didn't even have to say verbally. Eugene scooped the baby from Jamison's arms.

"Grandpa's man." He said as he looked down at him. Eugene cradled him like a football and Leah watched as her father bonded with her son. Everyone had gathered in the room like it was her first day at home, dotting over the baby. Even though Leah didn't really want to be bothered, she was still appreciative of the love that she was being given right now. It was going to be a long road ahead and as long as she had the love of these very people in the room, she knew she would be fine. Everyone stood and sat around for hours passing the baby around and talking. Leah eventually grew tired and leaned her head back into her pillow. Before she knew it, she was asleep and when she was done resting, she woke up to no one in the room but Jamison and their son. Jamison laid in a recliner chair that he had purchased for her room with his son laying on his chest sleeping. Leah couldn't do anything but smile at the sight of them. She closed her eyes and whispered a silent prayer. Praying that Jamison never got tired and lost patience with her. She knew he wouldn't because he said he wouldn't so Leah knew it to be true. If Jamison didn't do anything else, he always said what he meant and meant what he said. Leah closed her eyes and laid in bed lost in her thoughts as she continued to send prayers hoping that God answered not only one but all of them.

CHAPTER 24

*N*uNu and Tyson laid on the couch naked as they intertwined their fingers with one another. Ms. Andrea, NuNu's mother had offered to take the babies for the rest of the day after stopping to visit her. When they reached home the first thing they did was peel out of their clothes and attacked each other with sexual behavior like it was their first time indulging in one another. With Tyson and NuNu, it would always be like the first time because Tyson stayed bending her over in different ways that were unheard of.

Tyson stood and cracked his neck as he moved it from side to side.

"I'm about to go shower lor mama. I got something to handle at the club." Tyson announced.

NuNu nodded as she stayed sprawled on the couch. She couldn't move. Tyson left her weak but wanting more as if she could really take more right now. Tyson left her alone as he ascended the steps to go shower before he headed out. He wasn't gone five minutes before a knock on the door pulled NuNu from her sleep. She groaned.

KNOCK, KNOCK, KNOCK.

NuNu lifted from the couch lazily. She took her time putting on her clothes but the urgency in the knock this time put a little pep in her step.

KNOCK, KNOCK, KNOCK.

"I'm going to smack JJ ass as soon as I open this door." She said as she slid her shirt over her head.

NuNu took hurried steps toward the door and yanked it open without checking to see who it was because she already knew it was Jamison. When she pulled the door open NuNu looked as if she were seeing a ghost. Her eyes bulged from their sockets. She shook her head. This couldn't be happening. He was dead. Tyson had taken care of it, so she knew she had to be tripping.

"Dominic." She whispered.

Nicholas shook his head and smiled at her. He missed her like crazy and to be laying eyes on her melted his heart. His heart skipped a beat as he stared at her image. NuNu was just as beautiful as he remembered.

"I'm Nicholas NuNu. Dominic's little twin brother." He stated.

"Wha… What?" NuNu uttered in confusion.

"He has a twin?" She said more to herself than to him.

Nicholas nodded.

"He does Nu Marie."

NuNu looked at him in stun. *Nu Marie.* Only Dominic called her that. *What the fuck?* She thought. Nicholas smiled as he watched the confusion in her. He wanted to tell her his truth, but he couldn't bring himself to do it. He had heard that she moved on and now was a mother. He didn't want to disrupt her home. He loved her but he knew he couldn't have her. So, Nicholas sat his own feelings to the side and focused on the task at hand.

"I'm looking for Dominic. That's why I came here." He stated.

NuNu shrugged.

"I haven't seen him since the day he shot at my son's party." She whispered.

NuNu peered toward the stairs. She was praying like hell that Tyson wouldn't walk down the stairs and catch her talking to someone he thought was dead and someone she thought she was over. The sight of Nicholas had done something to her. Seeing his smooth chocolate face had sent her reminiscing back to two years ago. It was something different about Nicholas that sent a spark to her heart while in his vicinity. *Why the hell do I feel like this?* She pandered.

Nicholas noticed the look on her face and smirked. *She starting to remember.* He wanted desperately to explain but couldn't allow himself to.

"I'm sorry he did that Nu." Nicholas offered.

"Okay now that, that is out the way can you go now." NuNu whispered.

Nicholas knew she was checking to make sure her son's father wasn't coming. However, he wasn't scared of anyone. The only thing that scared him was the thought of not having NuNu. He had loved her but had to go away. He didn't think she would ever understand his reasoning so keeping it to himself was the best thing for both of them.

"You keep checking for your nigga like you scared of him or something."

NuNu shook her head.

"Could never, but if he catches you then it would be issues." NuNu shot back.

Nicholas swiped at his nose and then squared his shoulders.

"I didn't come here for all that. I just wanted to find out where my brother was and if anyone had seen him." He said.

"But I'm going to go and just know I love you, Nu Marie."

Nicholas leaned in and kissed NuNu. He had to. He

hadn't felt her lips in two years, and it didn't feel right not kissing her. NuNu's body betrayed her as she closed her eyes and allowed him to kiss her. She then snapped out of it and pushed him.

"What are you doing?" she yelled.

Nicholas feathered his lips.

"I'm sorry." He said.

Nicolas took a step back and then looked at NuNu one more time before turning to leave. He hadn't got the answers he was looking for, but he got to see the love of his life. The one he left behind. NuNu shut the door and then leaned her back against it. *His twin*, she thought in disbelief. She went to get her phone off the kitchen island because she had to tell Leah about what the hell just happened. Before she could get comfortable Tyson descended the steps bringing the smell of Curve with him. The smell of him intoxicated her until thoughts of Nicholas just leaving took her mind off his cologne.

Tyson stood in her face and kissed her. He kissed the same lips Nicholas had kissed not even 5 minutes ago. Guilt began to course through NuNu and she pulled back from the kiss.

"You better get going before we get something started." She said.

The doorbell rang and NuNu's heart froze. It literally stopped beating because she was so nervous. She just knew it was Nicholas again and she couldn't help but think the worst. Tyson strolled over to the door and looked out the peephole. He pulled the door open and the blood drained from his face.

"Who is it Ty?" NuNu asked.

Tyson didn't answer as he looked around trying to find out who could have left this haunting object on his front porch. Tyson grew nervous as he began to wonder what all this could mean. He was careful he knew he was careful. There was no one in sight so for all this to be taking place terrified him. *Did someone see me?* he thought. *Naw, I was careful, I know I was.* Now he was scared, and Tyson was the one nigga, that was not scared of anyone. However, Tyson was afraid that someone was playing games with him. Tyson looked down at the prosthetic leg and the picture of Mandy pinned to it.

"What the fuck?" he whispered.

DISCUSSION QUESTIONS

1. Do you think Tyson upholds NuNu and the things she does?
2. Is Jamison selfish for saying he is glad Stacy kept her promise and didn't have another child?
3. Was Stacy wrong for given Jamison up? How do you feel about the promise she made to him that day in the hospital?
4. Do you think Jamison forgave her only because of the circumstances?
5. Did Jamison leave Leah for too long and was his absence justified?
6. Why can't Marcus love Chrissy?
7. What made Chrissy believe that having Marcus son would make him love her or be with her?
8. How do you feel about the bond Jamison created with Leah's daughter? Was he out of line? Was it too soon? Did Stacy cross a line allowing them to officially meet without Leah's permission.
9. Will Jamison stay with Leah now that she is no longer who she was before the trauma?
10. Chels. Poor Chels. What are your thoughts about her and Jamison?

Made in United States
North Haven, CT
12 December 2021

12507030R00138